Deadly Yours

by

Cyndi L Stuart

A Samantha McMican Mystery

Dedication

I dedicate this book to the most voracious reader I know, my Aunt Jackie and to my very best friend and the love of my life, Kirk.

Prologue

June 19 - Chicago, IL

The wheels of the gurney clicked with each rotation on the polished linoleum floor. Lulled by the sound, a woman in green scrubs let her mind wander as she pushed the corpse to the double doors at the back of the county medical examiner's office. The funeral home van, with its engine running, waited in the halo of the streetlamp to take the body away. The young police detective yawned, tucked his cell phone back into his lapel pocket, pushed off from the wall by the door, and followed the gurney outside. The air, thick and damp, made it hard to breathe. The weather on his cell phone read ninety-five degrees with humidity to match. Sweat formed under his shirt collar, and the fabric darkened under his damp armpits. He pulled off his blazer.

The victim, an Alicia Alvarez, age fifty-seven, arrived from Northwestern Memorial yesterday. The examiner's office signed off on the release. With all the evidence collected and the crime scene processed, now the real legwork began.

The detective texted his boss a confirmation of the autopsy report and then sent a short note to his girlfriend. The late text would piss off Jasmine, but he lived in a state of confusion with her anyway, so better to err on the side of too much attention than not enough.

He looked up at the clear, dark sky then turned and walked west onto Harrison Street. The funeral van drove away in the opposite direction.

As he walked, his mind mulled over the case. *Someone gets killed while waiting to go* into *surgery? Huh, that's a new one. And strangled no less? Why not top her off with drugs? That would have delayed the investigation for days or may have never shown up as a murder at all.*

Either way, it meant endless early mornings and late nights into his foreseeable future. One day he would make captain and could be home with his feet up waiting for updates instead of sweating on the street at one in the morning.

When's that gonna happen? Another ten years?

Chapter 1

August 17 - Oregon

Long, slender fingers pulled on the blue nitrile gloves and secured them in place before opening the sealed package of creamy, yellow parchment paper. Bach's Mass in B Minor came from an iPod on a bookcase across the room. A voice hummed with the melody and then chuckled as the piece built to its crescendo.

"Perhaps an overly dramatic choice of music."

A hand placed a single sheet of parchment in the printer which sat alongside a carved teak desk. One of the gloved fingers clicked the mouse, and the printer began to purr. As the page printed, the fingers picked up a stick of red wax and held it over the flame of a tapered candle. The wax moved in the candlelight as it warmed. The red flowed off the stick like the velvet train of a dancer's skirt on its first swing across the ballroom. A large, gold signet ring stood beside an envelope addressed to a post office box.

"No mistakes this time. No one knows until I want them to know. No one finds the bodies until I want them to be found."

****

August 20 – Cove Beach, OR

If Samantha McMican knew she'd stop breathing

on Saturday, right before her fifty-fourth birthday, she would have packed up the few things she still called her own and run away, again. But because she didn't have this key piece of information about her future, she got up on what appeared to be an average Tuesday morning, slipped into her fuzzy wool slippers, pulled on an old pair of leggings, grabbed a baggy sweatshirt, and made her way to the kitchen.

She held the cup of strong, black tea to her lips as the hot liquid first bit her tongue and then slid down her throat like warm silk. A sigh escaped, joined by a slight smile. Her shoulders relaxed, and after one more sip, she moved from the kitchen, cup and saucer in hand, to the very small living room with a very large window. A cool breeze blew onshore, and through the open window drifted the scent of iodine and sea salt. The astringent smell nipped the back of her nose.

An enormous beachfront house blocked ninety-nine percent of the view due west and, with the help of two twenty-foot shore pines, kept her cottage in almost constant shadow. In the sweet spot, she stood and stared out at the small sliver of the Pacific Ocean through the window.

From her old, portable CD player the deep, throaty voice of Gaye Adegbalola filled the room with the blues and broken hearts. Samantha hummed as she pulled herself away from the window and over to the laptop on her little dining room table. She confirmed the final edit, typed a short note to her client, attached the document with the final invoice, and with a click it disappeared. She sighed again and turned back toward the window. *Finally!* she thought, *Done with that exercise in boredom. Now the rest of the summer is mine.*

For the thousandth time she told herself not every freelance project needed to be interesting. It just needed to pay the bills. If she turned down every research job due to extreme lack of interest, she'd find herself unemployed. When she received the final check, then the four-month slog through the history of the American Revolution for a best-selling author would be worth it.

The problem sat in her own lap, not the writer's. She just didn't find the subject all that riveting. Not like the research she used to do.

And, said a faint voice in her head, *the choice you made when you ran away.*

"You're looking serious this morning, darling," said a voice with a distinct British accent.

Startled, Sam jerked her eyes from the view and turned toward the old, two-story, saltbox house with cedar shake siding, and cobalt-blue shutters. She scanned the yard for her landlady.

"Aunt Dot? Where are you?"

"Over here, dear," said the eighty-three-year-old as she pulled herself up from her flower bed and appeared above the picket fence. "Just getting some weeding out of the way."

She pointed to the cup in Samantha's hand.

"What's in the pot this morning?"

"The Burmese black tea you turned me on to."

"Oh, lovely."

Dorothy Dixon, known by the locals as Aunt Dot, took off her sandy garden gloves and pushed aside a strand of long white hair with the back of her hand.

"Bring your cup over. I'll put a tray together and

meet you on the deck."

Sam checked the time on her cell phone. "Sorry, I only have fifteen minutes. Got to jump in the shower."

"Deadline day!" said both Samantha and Aunt Dot at the same time.

"At least come over and take a piece or two of the zucchini bread I made last night before you head to work." Dorothy didn't wait for an answer.

Sam called out before the woman slipped away. "Hold on. Didn't you volunteer at the historical society all weekend? When did you have time to bake zucchini bread?"

"Oh, there's always time for what you want." As she disappeared out of sight, she added, "And, as you know, zucchini and tides wait for no woman."

Sam walked around the corner of Dorothy's beach house toward the deck and stopped. Her breath caught in her throat. The entire Pacific Ocean shone in front of her. The bright August sunshine turned the water a deep blue and made the waves a crisp white. Frothy bubbles churned and stuck to the sand. High waves smacked the black basalt walls of the three large monoliths standing offshore and shot skyward as if fired from a cannon.

She stepped up onto the deck. "The surf is really rockin' today."

"Yes, maybe there's a storm coming in."

Sam narrowed her gaze and looked out at the sea. "Hmm, nothing on the horizon. No dark clouds. But a storm would be nice to chase the tourists away."

"Quite nice." Aunt Dot leaned over the table and sliced the sweet bread.

"But it's going to mean some extra cleaning for your pool."

Dorothy looked over her shoulder at the clear water in the small exercise pool at the end of the deck. Her husband, Norman, put it in after his knee surgery ten years ago. She lost her "dearest Norman" a few months before Sam moved to Cove Beach. Dorothy still used the pool every day.

"Hmm, might be right about that...to chase away the crowds, it'll be worth it."

Aunt Dot turned back and looked at the blue and white polka dot cup in Sam's hand. She frowned and said, "Oh, what on earth are you doing with that horrible tea mug?"

Sam raised her mug in salute and grinned. "These are the dishes in my cupboard. You'll have to talk to the landlady if you're unhappy about it."

"It's maddening!"

"Well, if you're going to furnish my cottage with nothing but polka dots, what's a woman to do?"

This discussion started three years ago, when Sam moved into the little house. As she pulled out drawers and opened cabinets on her first day, she found polka dots of all colors and sizes plastered on everything. She stood in the kitchen and laughed out loud. Polka dot tea towels, pillows, dishes, trivets, blankets, and rugs filled the cottage. *Ha!* she thought at the time, *must be deliberate.*

"I can't have those hideous things in my house."

"Oh, I see. Just in my house. You know, you could just tell people you don't like polka dots. That might solve your problem."

Aunt Dot's head swung from side to side. "No, no, no. When people give you things, you must be polite."

Back in her cottage, Sam showered and pulled on a

pair of faded old jeans lying in a heap by the bed. With a piece of zucchini bread held between her teeth, she pushed her arms through a light cotton shirt. A small chime came from the cell phone on the nightstand. Sam scooped it up and read a text.

—*Drinks @ Dave's 6pm? V, M, U & Me*—

Sam smiled and started to type back to Kim Wallis, the north coast's only resident anthropologist and one of the book clubbers she met at Crooked House Books. Then she stopped. She accepted all past invitations to meet at Dave's Tavern. Why did she hesitate this time? She shook her head and continued typing.

—*Sure. See you then.*—

She slipped her bare feet into her Birkenstocks and flung a leather rucksack onto her shoulder. Out through the wooden gate, she walked away from her tiny house and down the dune into town.

Even at nine in the morning, the town buzzed with tourists headed to the beach or staring into the windows of closed gifts shops. Only the Beach House Bakery, the small grocery store, and coffee shops opened before ten. Sam dodged a large group of people walking five abreast on the sidewalk and ducked into the alley that led to the backside of the post office. After opening two post office boxes, she jammed the stack of work mail and her personal mail into her backpack and headed toward an old clapboard-sided building in the middle of town.

A handful of shops, devoted to and dependent on all those tourists, lined the ground floor of the closest thing the town had to a mall. A clothing shop filled the first storefront with beach wear designed for sunny southern California beaches. Sam noticed the string bikini on the mannequin in the window with a matching pair of flip-flops. A perfect fit if Cove Beach sat south of Malibu, not in Oregon. A hot summer day in this northern town topped out at seventy-three degrees. Always a quick study, Sam now kept a fleece jacket and a raincoat within reach year-round.

She passed by the two more sensible shops, local pottery and saltwater taffy, and walked to the back of the building. A shabby sign with peeling white paint read *The Cove Beach Chronicle*. It hung alongside a small door which led up a steep and narrow flight of stairs.

The familiar odor of beach mold, old carpet, and fresh coffee hit her in the face as she walked into the newsroom. Mike Campbell, owner and editor of the paper, sat with his head hidden behind a computer screen. His broad shoulders peeked out from either side of the monitor as his fingers flew across the keyboard.

"Legion meeting last night. Went late."

Those few words told Sam all she needed to know. Mike stayed after the monthly American Legion Hall meeting for one drink that turned into too many drinks. With a nod Sam moved to her desk and dropped her backpack on the floor by her swivel chair.

Mike got up and walked toward the coffee pot. The coffee maker, electric kettle, and small fridge all sat along the far wall in their makeshift kitchenette. As Sam watched the syrupy black liquid drop into his mug, she stayed silent. Mike's wife, Joy, battled to get Mike to cut back on the coffee. Last month, at the Legion's open-mic night, Joy took Sam aside and asked her to stop him after two cups when they worked in the office together. She gave Joy a noncommittal murmur and changed the subject as fast as possible. Sam figured, at seventy-two, Mike earned the right to enjoy a few vices. And she knew couple-trouble when she saw it. Her little part-time job didn't pay enough to jump into the middle of that debate.

"What have you got for me, kid?"

Sam rolled the cursor down through the articles on her laptop as she read them off to Mike.

"To edit, I have ready the backyard gardens tour for the *Garden Gate* section, along with the *Plant of the Week* contribution by Meg. I picked up *The Book Nook* column from Vicki...um... my *A Bird's-Eye View* piece on the nesting tufted puffins...and let's see...oh, yes...interviews about the declining numbers of common murres...all are coming to you right now."

Mike grunted his thanks, and she turned toward the flashing red light on their old nineteen eighties multiline phone. She hit the speaker button and waited with pen and paper for the first message.

"Sam? CC! Call when you get a chance!"

Samantha's whole body went still. Cornelia Cowan.

The next message played.

"Sam, CC again. I know I'm not supposed to contact you, unless...*shit!*...just call me."

Droplets of sweat formed on her upper lip, and her body shivered. She pulled out her cell phone. The words on her lock screen read, *Emergency Calls Only*. No cell signal.

The message light still flashed. She hit the button, and CC's voice cried out.

"Sam, I'm so sorry. Have you checked your mail? God, I fucked up. I hope I'm wrong. Call me."

Mike poked his head from around the computer. "That sounds serious."

Silence.

Mike's brows furrowed when he caught sight of her pale face. "Hey, kid, what's up?"

Samantha's hands shook as she reached for her rucksack. It took three tries to get the zipper to move. She turned the whole bag upside down onto her desk. Pens clattered and rolled off onto the floor, her wallet slid across the desk, and mail landed in a pile.

Mike stood up. "What in the hell?"

Samantha reached out and grabbed the metal letter opener. She held the handle tight in her hand like a knife. With the tip, she moved each piece of mail aside. There, tucked partway under an ad for better cell service, lay a red wax seal. A seal with the imprint of a capital letter "'M'" pressed into yellow parchment paper.

Sam winced, her hand jerked, and the opener clattered to the floor. White lights danced and twinkled along the edges of her vision. The sounds around her faded. Mike's lips moved as he walked toward her, but a small buzzing filled her ears. Sam leaned forward over her desk and fanned out her hands, palms pressed into the wooden surface.

She shook her head back and forth. Bile filled the back of her throat.

"No, no, no," she whispered, "not again, not again. I'm safe here."

Images of dead strangers swam in front of her face. She sobbed, "Oh, for fuck's sake, stay focused! You can't faint now."

Her eyes fluttered downward. Her outstretched

hands no longer held her weight. The buzzing in her ears turned to complete silence.

"Samantha!" Mike shouted. He took two quick strides and reached out. "Oh, son of a bitch!"

Before her head hit the top of her desk, she thought, *The killer is back.*

Chapter 2

August 20 – Cove Beach, OR

Samantha walked into the bottom of a curved, deep lecture hall. "The Pit" the students called it. As she looked up at the 220 alert faces terraced above her, she felt a vibration in her belly and her face flush. Her hands shook with a slight tremble, followed by a flip in her stomach. The familiar nauseous excitement she felt right before she spoke those first few words in front of large groups of people never failed to show up on the first day of the fall term.

She tapped her notes together on the podium.

"Good morning, I'm Professor Morrill, and this is Lit. 260, The Art of Detection. Over the next sixteen weeks, we are going to look at the last two-hundred and fifty years of killers, crimes, and the literature influenced by true-life events or true-life events that may have been influenced by..."

She had given this first lecture so many times over the years, she joked with colleagues that she felt like a doll with a string at the back. "Just pull the string and off I go." But today didn't look right. The students moved as if behind a plate of lead glass, distorted, then clear, and then distorted again. And the professor heard her name being called over and over, each time a little louder.

The early morning light glowed in the windows at the back of the room. The warmth from the filled auditorium moved over her body. As she turned toward the whiteboard, she saw movement on the ground out of the corner of her left eye. A line of blood flowed toward her foot. She raised her head and saw three bodies, all students, lying on the bright, white linoleum floor with their heads covered in blood alongside a little brown and white spotted dog. The little dog's throat gaped wide from straight, deep cuts.

"Sam?" said a voice by the door.

"Who's calling me?"

"Sam!"

"Mike Campbell? He doesn't belong here—"

"*Samantha!*" said Mike. His voice rose louder each time he called her name. His quick strides got him to the desk just in time to catch Samantha's head before it hit the top. In one quick motion, Mike sat Sam down in the swivel chair and took her forehead in his large left hand. With his right across her shoulders, he bent her head to rest between her knees. Sam started to mumble a few unintelligible words.

"Christ on a crutch," he said, with a long exhale. "You could have broken your nose."

Mike rubbed Sam's back in small circles like he used to do for his youngest when she woke up with nightmares. She shivered at his touch. The warmth she felt moments before disappeared as the floor came into focus. His knee braced her leg against the chair. She smelled the mustiness of the old office and the spiciness of his aftershave.

Mike leaned in to hear her next words.

"I'm okay."

"Like hell you are. Now, just wait right here. All right? Can you hold yourself up?"

Sam nodded and mumbled, "This is nice. I'll just stay like this for a while."

He pushed her and the chair up closer to the desk and went back over to the far wall. He jerked open drawers in the cabinet under the coffee maker. Now, with a dish towel in hand, he turned on the sink and pushed it under the stream of cold water. His large hands wrung out the fabric until it shook from the force. He walked back to Sam and placed the cool towel on the back of her neck. When she tried to move, he commanded her to stay still.

Then, calmer than before, he said, "Just give it a minute."

After a few more moments, she sat up. Mike went to the counter and returned with a can of cola from the mini fridge. As he walked back, he popped the tab on the top and put the cold can in Sam's hand.

"Drink this, and then we'll talk." Mike put his hand up as Sam started to reply. He pointed at the can. "After you take a swig of that first."

Samantha took first a small sip and then a long drink of the cold bubbly soda. As it hit the back of her throat, the nausea began to recede. Another swallow and she could sit up a little straighter. The room still moved in and out of focus, so she pressed her elbows into the top of the desk to stay steady. When she closed her eyes, she could still make out the bodies on the classroom floor, but as the moments passed the images faded. Vivid memories from five years before flooded in and took their place.

Mike rolled his own desk chair over beside hers.

He again braced her chair with his knee to keep it steady. "So, what in the hell is this all about?"

Samantha forced her eyes up to his and then turned her gaze to the off-white envelope now sitting on the top of the stack with its red seal facing up. She reached out a hand and pointed to the letter, but when Mike reached for it, she yelled out, "Stop!"

Mike jumped and pulled his hand back as if caught in a mousetrap. She put her hand on Mike's big forearm with a chuckle and shook her head.

"Sorry, I didn't mean to shout and freak you out. Just don't touch it. It will need to be dusted for prints. It won't do any good, but they'll want them all the same."

At that, Mike jerked his head to stare at her with raised eyebrows and eyes wide. "Prints?"

"And I need to make a call." She rested her head in her left hand and rubbed her temple. Then she remembered CC's desperate message and added, "I need to make two calls."

An hour later, three calls had been made and she sat face-to-face with the Cove Beach Chief of Police, Marlene Porter. When Samantha began to explain, the newsroom went silent.

Chapter 3

August 20 – Portland, OR

It had only been forty-eight hours, right? Detective Jessica Noguchi thought as she reviewed her notes in her mind. *A body found folded up inside an old sea trunk—neighbors confirmed a house party two nights before—owner, Robert Brignone, hadn't been seen since.*

As she navigated the cramped streets in Arlington Heights an hour before, she knew this wouldn't be an easy case. Brignone lived just north of Portland's famous Japanese Gardens in one of the more expensive areas of the city. The old, established neighborhood grew in stature every year as the city's population exploded. Each house represented a different era—colonial, saltbox, art nouveau, craftsman, and many more Jess couldn't identify.

"A million-dollar house there, two-point-five mil there. Nothing but money," Jessica muttered as she turned onto SW Fairview Avenue for the third time. "This better be the right goddamn road."

Fairview snaked and ambled through the neighborhood and seemed to go every which way. As she drove around the corner, the road widened and the nineteen-thirties red brick and stucco, Tudor-inspired home came into view. The driveway filled with cop cars confirmed she'd found the crime scene.

Now in the victim's study, she could see the cause of death looked tricky. She stood a safe six feet away from the body and leaned her long torso in to get a better look. Her black ponytail, bound at the nape of her neck with a wide, colorful blue and yellow printed headband, fell forward onto her shoulder. The wound appeared to be in the abdomen but obscured by the legs and upper chest as the two came together. Jess turned away and tossed the rebel hair onto her back. The wait for the medical examiner's analysis left her antsy for answers. Just then Jess glanced up to see Colin Davies enter the scene covered in protective gear.

She called out, "Colin, I could use your help over here."

A compact man with graying sandy brown hair looked up from his cell phone and walked over to her. He stood five-foot-eight, and Jessica put him in his late forties.

"I was just looking over the photos you sent." Colin's British accent caused a few of the crime scene detectives to turn toward the sound of his voice. He didn't notice as he stared at the body lying in the sea trunk. "Was he packaged for shipment?"

Jessica rolled her eyes and shook her head.

"I'm not taking the piss," he said. "It could be a viable way to remove the body, and no one would be the wiser for several days."

She smiled at the profiler. She shook her head again and assumed "piss" meant something different in England. "Except for the blood that would have leaked all over the back of the frickin' mail truck!"

Unfazed, Colin moved in closer to the body. "Ah,

right, that's the lining of the trunk I was seeing in the photo. No plastic surrounding the body then? So, the killer wanted the body found, if not immediately, then within a day or two."

"Appears so, yes." Jess then turned to the room and asked, "So, Calhoun, what have we got?"

Jacob Calhoun, a tall, young officer, walked over to the detective and said, "Aside from what we already know about Robert Brignone, age fifty-nine and editor of the *Northwest News Tribune*, he threw one of these parties every year for friends, family, and VIPs around town."

"Married? Dating?"

"Twice divorced. First one a wife, second one a husband."

When Jacob didn't continue, Jess looked up and shrugged. "So, he's gay or bi. Move on."

"Right, it's not that." Jacob flipped through the notes on his phone. "It looks like he might have hooked up with someone at the end of the party. The caterers thought there might have been someone in the house with Brignone when they were packing up. They heard people talking in the room off the kitchen."

"Great, track it down."

"Yes, ma'am. Already on it. I put out the word to those still interviewing guests and those canvassing the neighborhood. If he was dating someone or hooked up at the party, we'll know soon enough."

Over the low buzz of the crime scene, Jess felt her cell phone vibrate in her pocket. The detective frowned at the number.

"Noguchi here," Jess said as she turned away from Colin to answer the call. "AJ? Hey, it's been a while—

of course, what can I—" She paused, listened, and then said, "*Oh, fuck!*"

At that, everyone at the crime scene turned and stared. She waved them all back to work.

"Ok, here's what I need you to do." She kept the phone to her ear and walked into the kitchen away from the body. Everyone turned back to their tasks.

As Colin moved around the trunk, he ran through all the possible scenarios in his head. He focused on the mind of the killer and their intentions. But, as he knew, sometimes a body in a trunk is just a body in a trunk. Sometimes convenience wins over tactics when a killer gets rushed or panicked.

The careful placement of the body and arrangement of the arms and legs told him this killer didn't panic. The tingle on the back of his neck couldn't be a coincidence. He knew this scene, but he just couldn't put his finger on how he knew it. Colin glanced up to see Jessica return to the study with a face like thunder.

"Everything all right?"

"No. And, if what I just heard is true, we are in for a shitstorm."

She pinched the bronze skin between her eyebrows and closed her eyes. Colin remained silent. She looked up a moment later with her eyes fixed on the crime scene.

"Okay. Colin, I need you to return to the station with me and," she said as her eyes searched around the room, "Calhoun? I need you to stay here and oversee the rest of the evidence collection, neighbor interviews—you get it—call me with hourly reports."

Jess walked to the door with Colin. As they moved outside and got into her unmarked car, Colin asked,

"How bad is it?"

"Let's just say, criminal profiler, you're going to earn what little we pay you on this one." She rammed the car into reverse and bolted backward out of the driveway.

Chapter 4

August 21 – Hwy 26, OR

On any other day, the drive inland along scenic Sunset Highway would have been beautiful. But today Samantha's mind spun as she fidgeted in the passenger seat of Marlene Porter's SUV. She didn't know the chief very well and anticipated an awkward drive to Portland.

The inside of the police vehicle did little to help her anxiety. She sat perched amongst computer screens, radios, and buttons. Sam didn't know where to put her arms when she first got into the car. Everything looked important and breakable.

Marlene smiled and started the engine. "Not to worry. You can't hurt a thing. Although, I don't let many civilians or rookie cops ride in my rig."

"I can see why. It looks like the bridge of the *USS Enterprise* in here."

The six-foot-tall, dark-haired police chief took her hand off the wheel and turned toward Sam with her right eyebrow raised. "Did you just make a Star Trek reference?"

Sam, who had her head down to buckle her seat belt, glanced up to see Marlene's sardonic expression. Sam couldn't resist holding up her hand and spreading out her fingers left to right into a V. "Live long and prosper?" They both laughed.

Now on the road, Marlene went on to ease Samantha's mind about the investigation. "It is an understatement to say these last two days have been crap for you, and it won't get much better. You are going to relive it all over again when we get to Portland, so let's put this away for the moment."

The tension in Sam's shoulders released, and the two women relaxed into small talk. After yesterday's talk in *The Chronicle* office, the chief now knew the basics of the killings which precipitated her move to Cove Beach but not all the details. When she called Jess the day the letter arrived, Jess asked how long the chief of police had been with the local office. Once Sam said ten years, Jess told her to talk only to Chief Porter and no one else about the previous killings. She promised to get in touch once she returned to the station and talked to her boss.

After Jessica met with her bureau chief, she and Marlene discussed the letter and a plan for Samantha's safety. Marlene and Sam would drive into the Portland police station first thing in the morning with the evidence. Since the letter came to Sam's new identity in Cove Beach, both Marlene and Jessica urged Sam not to go home, not until their meeting tomorrow.

Mike jumped in. "She's staying with me and Joy tonight."

"No!" Sam shook her head. "I'm—"

Before Sam could argue, Mike's large hand went up and he said in a firm, clear tone that would have brought a packed stadium to a standstill, "It's done!"

The office went silent. Sam crossed her arms and gritted her teeth. Her next words came out with more force than she intended. "Okay! Fine! I know when I'm beat."

The rest of the day and night went by in a haze of activity mixed with brief moments of solitude as others discussed her fate. Jessica decided she couldn't tell Mike and Joy the full story. This came even after Sam explained the Campbells moved to Cove Beach over eight years ago from Chicago and she had not met either one of them before living in town. Jess understood but told her to hold off until both police departments knew what they were up against.

"Look, I'm sure he's a good guy," Jessica said, "but remember he is still the owner and editor of a newspaper." Marlene agreed.

While Mike got the Wednesday edition to the printer, she spent the afternoon at the police station. Then she was off to the Campbells' in the north end of town to stay the night. Cove Beach consisted of small, old cabins scattered on the back streets and large, elaborate homes along the beachfront dune. But off the first entrance into town the locals call North Beach, a group of five buildings didn't fit. As they entered the nineteen-eighties development of condos, Sam noted four units in each building all with ocean views. Mike and Joy had a top unit in the middle of building B.

As they sat down to dinner, Sam's phone chimed. She pulled it out of her pocket.

—Where are u? Your drink is waiting and so are we.—

"Oh, no."

Mike looked up at Sam with a frown. "Everything okay?"

"Sorry. Yes. I just forgot about the book clubbers. I

was supposed to meet them for drinks tonight. Give me a minute."

Sam walked away from the table and texted Kim back.

—So sorry, something came up. 1st round—next time—on me.—

Sam then texted Aunt Dot with an excuse just as vague. She knew when her neighbor didn't see the lights on in the cottage she would worry and call in the National Guard. As she hit send, another text came through from Meg Hadley.

—R U getting laid? Send pics! No? Better be a damn good reason for standing us up, sweet pea!—

She smiled and tucked her phone into her back pocket before either of the two Campbells caught a glimpse of the local nursery owner's message. Then the phone went off for a third time. She hoped to see a call from CC, but instead a text from Vicki Mathews, the owner of Crooked House Books, appeared.

—Ignore Meg, she's already drunk. Hope you are okay. Talk soon. x—

She sat back down with Mike to her right and Joy across from her at their dining room table. With the unmentionable monster in the room, Sam braced herself for the awkward pauses and stilted conversation. But after a few minutes of small talk, Mike and Joy's plan became clear. The two of them, married for more than forty years, didn't miss a beat when they launched into those tales all couples tell. They talked about their college days, how they met, the stories Mike used to cover for the newspaper in Chicago, their two daughters, and their next trip to see the grandkids.

Right after they had cleared the table and sat down

in the living room, a new text came through from Kim.

—Hey, Ted just came in with Gordon—why is there a police car parked at your house? Meg wants to know if you got busted for solicitation again?—

Before Sam could answer, another text came through.

No, seriously—r u all right?—

She texted back.

—I'm fine. Just Aunt Dot sunbathing in the nude. 3rd strike so they r probably there to take her in.—

Mike saw the grin on Sam's face and asked, "What's all that about?"

Sam looked up from her cell. "Oh, it's just the book clubbers again. Looks like half the town already knows something's up." She went on to tell them about the text and the police car.

Mike snorted. "That's small towns for you. Can't fart without the neighbors knowing."

"Mike!" said Joy as she picked up a copy of *Oregon Coast* magazine off the coffee table and threw it at him. She then turned to Samantha. "He thinks he's so funny. The old goat."

Everyone's cells stayed quiet the rest of the night, and she felt a lot better than she anticipated when she went off to bed. Then she turned out the light. With nothing to think about but the letter and the killer, her mind refused to stay still.

The glow of her cell phone stared at her in the darkness. It showed five bars and full coverage, but no new messages.

Through the open window a soft breeze blew in, and for the first time in her life the sound of the waves brought no comfort. She rolled onto her side and curled her knees into her belly. Her heart ached in her chest. She rubbed her fingers into her sternum to try and stop the pain.

The faint voice in her head asked, *How far away can you run this time?*

Chapter 5

August 21 – Portland, OR

"We've found the weapon," said a voice on the other end of the early morning call to Jessica from the Crime Scene Unit.

"Right on! Where and what is it?'"

Her cell reception crackled as she passed through the tunnel by the zoo on Hwy 26. She took this route to the station to avoid the Burnside morning traffic. As she hit the brakes, she imagined that damn Davies already at his desk. The college put him in some fancy townhouse on Park Street a few blocks from headquarters. She exhaled a long sigh. At least when she did arrive, she could walk in with something new to report.

"It is a twenty-inch-long sword, maybe antique, maybe a copy, hidden behind the big bureau in the study." The officer on the other end of the phone sketched out the facts. "We thought the cabinet was mounted flush to the wall until we got a good look. The sword is bagged and headed to the lab."

Just the break we needed, she thought as she lurched through the city to the Portland Police Bureau parking lot. Once at the station, she bounded up the stairs two at a time until she arrived at the third-floor homicide department. When she walked through the door and clocked Colin perched on his temporary desk flipping through reports, she stopped and took a deep cleansing Lamaze breath. *If only that Brit had two screaming kids to get on the bus every morning, he might not look so smug.*

Engrossed in the medical examiner's report on the man's body found in the trunk, Colin didn't see Jess enter the room. As he flipped through the pages, he marveled at how fast the report had come through. The autopsy request moved to the front of the queue, once the victim was identified as the editor and chief of the second largest newspaper in Oregon, *The Northwest News Tribune*.

As Colin focused on the results, certain phrases stuck out.

Stabbed through the abdomen with great force, back to front

Abdominal aorta severed

Victim would have lost consciousness in approximately 20 seconds

Loss of blood and life in two to four minutes

Weapon: narrow blade greater than 18 inches long, smooth, possible sword

Death likely occurred within trunk

Body manipulated after death into the folded position found in trunk

Death occurred approximately 48-52 hours prior to discovery

Colin's mind began to turn. He confirmed the absence of defensive wounds yesterday at the scene. He knew the easiest way to coerce someone into a trunk would be at gunpoint. All other methods took either a smooth talker or drugs, and no drugs, not even aspirin, were found in the victim's system. Alcohol showed on the tox-screen but not enough to impair his mind or body.

As he stared at the report, his mind wandered through past cases. Nothing. He couldn't find a specific memory of this crime scene, but something still pulled on him. A familiarity. *So, bugger, what was it?*

Jess stood by Colin's desk and waited. She could see the gears turning in his head. Yes, his punctuality and good manners needled her, but to work with the best profiler of the day seemed a fair trade.

She disliked all the other profilers she'd met. She found them to be arrogant assholes who believed the sun rose and set with their brilliance and the idiot cops just went out with the arrest warrant once the profiler solved the case. Maybe they just turned them out differently in England, she didn't know, but Colin did his job, asked good questions, listened to the officers on the case, and held his tongue until his analysis reflected a complete picture of the case. She didn't want to think about how much she would miss him around the office when he left to lecture at a university in Portland in a few weeks. Because of this, she stood there with her arms crossed and let him think. She didn't shout him to attention as she would have done to her own detectives.

Out of the corner of his eye, Colin glanced down at a pair of black leather shoes. His head snapped up. "Oh, Detective! I was just thinking about your nutter and the body he or she left in the trunk."

As Colin eyes now settled on Jessica's face, he couldn't imagine why she looked so cross at only eight fifteen in the morning.

"And what do you think?"

Colin hesitated. He presented educational training to detectives in basic profiling techniques, and his work on this current case came down to the department and Jessica's goodwill.

"Um, well, this is your party. I'm just along for the ride, but I do have a few thoughts if you…?" His voice trailed off, as he waited for her okay to continue.

He didn't want to overstep his role. Profiling had become a touchy subject, and the term "profile" had started to mean something different than its original purpose intended. This type of profile didn't single someone out by their race, geography, or economic status. A profile gave the detective team a psychological idea of what the killer might be like. Nothing more, nothing less, regardless of what someone might see on TV. While some human characteristics fit in a corresponding box, others didn't. Colin found the idea of understanding someone's behavior before ever meeting them bloody brainless. But certain killers followed certain patterns, all of which depended on their upbringing and background. That's where profiling worked to catch them before they could kill again.

Jess nodded for Colin to continue. In the next hour they went over scenarios, possible profiles, possible motives, and the details of the scene. They both agreed the weapon gave them a good break, but until the forensics came back on the sword, they weren't much further along than when they started.

Jessica looked up from her notes. "You said he or she at the crime scene. Do you think we could be looking for a woman?"

"There's nothing to indicate male or female, at the

moment, only that statistically it's more likely to be a man—white male, thirty-five to fifty years old. But I never want to rule out sex, race, or those sorts of attributes this early. Coercing someone into a sea trunk isn't the purview of only a male killer. A man or a woman could do it with a gun, seduction, or cajoling. And I think we can both agree, pushing a sharp sword through once the victim is locked inside is anyone's game."

"Running someone through with a sword, hmm, seems personal, doesn't it?"

"Right," he said and looked toward the incident wall across the room. "That's the tricky bit. I—"

Just then Jessica's phone chimed. "Whoa-up." She glanced over at the text and then at Colin. "Hold that thought. They're here."

As they moved away from the desk toward the conference room, Colin debated if he should tell her about his déjà vu at the crime scene. With a shake of his head, he decided to stay mum for the time being. *One nutter at a time*, he thought.

Colin's experience on the job dispelled the TV and movie idea of the cop's "gut" years ago. Most cops achieved success by good, solid police work. Instinct played a small role in the end. The real work happened through the daily drudgery of interviews, tracking down leads, and knowing when someone was feeding you a load of bollocks. Experience gave the illusion of instinct.. Cops and profilers learned to trust their experience.

Chapter 6

August 21 – Police Bureau, Portland, OR

As Marlene and Sam entered police headquarters in downtown Portland, they found themselves stopped by a small squad of armed officers. Marlene showed her badge to the first officer by the door. The officer nodded and directed Sam to one line and Marlene to a separate area off to the left where two other officers waited with handheld metal detectors. Before she walked away, Marlene leaned over and whispered to Sam, "Because I'm in uniform, I can't pass through the detectors. I'd light that thing up like a slot machine."

Sam placed her purse, keys, and cell phone into a plastic tub and watched the conveyor belt carry them away. Once cleared, they both made their way to a large desk in the middle of the entrance hall. Marlene checked them in at reception and gave Detective Noguchi's name. As the receptionist made the call to the homicide office, Sam and Marlene went to find chairs along the wall.

"That was intense," said Sam.

"It's from all the riots. City stations are all on edge."

Sam took out her phone and tried to reach CC again. There had been no answer to the multiple texts and messages she left on her friend's phone. When

Marlene contacted Jessica the day before, she asked if a patrol team might check Cornelia Cowan's office and apartment.

With her head against the faux wood wall, Sam closed her eyes and saw CC's face. Cornelia left the New York publishing world just a few years before they met to try and save Duniway College's small, floundering book publishing business, Upton Press.

Even after years of living in the Pearl District, the most expensive condo area of Oregon's largest city, CC never succumbed to Portlandia's fashion or attitude. The laid-back approach toward life, clothing, and questionable hygiene infuriated her. At least once a week, after driving the forty minutes from Portland to Chinook, you could hear her mutter under her breath, "Why in the hell did I ever agree to move to this hippy-revival-commune slash yuppie stronghold?"

Sam's mind shifted back to their first meeting. At the time, she taught The Art of Detection at Duniway College. Throughout the semester, she covered everything from the Ratcliff Highway Murders to *Moonstone* and Jack the Ripper, Dorothy Sayers and Agatha Christie, James Patterson and Elizabeth George, and ended with the renewed fascination with Sherlock Holmes. Each term the class moved to bigger and bigger classrooms. In year three it found a permanent place in the college's largest lecture hall, "The Pit." It grew to become the second most popular class in the catalog. The sex education class nicknamed "dirty 230" still held the number one spot. When friends kidded her about second place, she would laugh and say, "Are you nuts? I'd sign-up for 'dirty 230' before some old English Lit class too."

All this popularity caught the attention of Cornelia and led to a surprise message on Sam's office phone. The editor wanted her to write her own textbook for the course. Sam couldn't help being a little flattered and more than curious, so they set a date to meet.

"What in the hell are you wearing?" came the first words out of CC's mouth as she watched a sweaty, forty-something woman walk into her office.

Sam stopped short in the doorway to the editor's office. She arrived in her usual summer attire. She wore a tank top with a short-sleeved cotton shirt over it to hide her chubby upper arms, stretchy cotton capris to allow for her ever advancing and retreating waistline, well-worn sandals, and a rucksack on her back. Late July brought hot, muggy weather and rendered any makeup a waste of time. So, Sam didn't bother to wear any.

"Did you just mug a bag lady in the park on your way over here?" the tall publisher asked, as she sat with legs crossed in a sleek, black, size-two designer suit and three-inch stilettos. Sam only had a moment to decide how to respond. *Aha*, a thought came to her in a flash, *smartass begets smartass*. Sam held her head high, smiled, and walked into the office.

"We traded." Her eyes glinted as she dropped her backpack into one of chairs by the rude woman's desk. "But my feet were too big, so I had to keep my own shoes. She didn't seem that disappointed really. Maybe a little too crunchy granola for her."

Sam and CC both stared down at her sunburned, Birkenstock-clad feet. Cornelia looked dazed. Then she threw her head back and cackled. People in the hallway turned and stared. She called Sam a sarcastic bitch, told her how much she liked her, hated her clothes, and asked what the fuck she was doing here with all these shithead academics.

Two more different people could not be found, but that's how a decades-long friendship began and endured. While she worked to get her textbook published and out on the market, CC encouraged her to write her own mystery novel.

"Look," the editor said to Samantha during their first meeting. "I know that group you're working with over in the Lit department. No street smarts in the whole bunch, except maybe that reporter from *The Tribune*. He at least comes from the real world. The rest? Just too focused on dusty old tomes to see that the world has moved on.

"Yes, yes." She waved her hand at Sam when she tried to interrupt. "The classics are important, but what you're doing with this Art of Detection thing, now that's cutting edge. Might as well capitalize on it and write a mystery of your own."

Did this one choice lead to the first killings? No one could say for sure.

Sam jumped as she felt fingers on her arm. "Sorry." Marlene pulled back her hand. "Didn't mean to scare you. You didn't hear me the first time. Detective Noguchi is on her way down."

Just then the tall detective appeared at the top of the stairs. Sam pointed her out to Marlene. As the two women reached the bottom of the staircase, Jessica reached out and took Sam's right hand and held it in both of hers. "AJ, I'm so sorry."

Marlene's eyes moved to Sam's face when Jess called her "AJ." This new revelation for the chief still needed to sink in. Jessica, whom she hadn't seen or talked to in four and a half years, looked like Sam remembered but with a touch of gray woven into her black hair. She thought for a moment. *If I'm going to turn fifty-four, then she must be, what? Forty?* With a gentle squeeze before she let go, Jess went on, "We're going to get the asshole this time."

"Is there any word about CC, Cornelia Cowan? The friend who called and left me the messages," Sam asked as they walked up the stairs.

"We've confirmed she didn't go to her office yesterday nor has she shown up there today."

"But those messages came in yesterday before ten a.m., and that would mean she's—"

"Now, wait!" said Jess as she put her hand up to stop the long list of questions. "According to her office, at the time she called you, she would have still been in Chicago for a conference, coming back this morning, landing in about an hour, and before you ask, she knows I have a patrol car waiting at the airport to pick her up and bring her here."

Once in the homicide office, Jess led them to a conference room. A man in crisp sky-blue shirt and navy blazer rose from a chair on the far side of a long table. She introduced both Sam and Chief Porter to Colin Davies as a criminal profiler on temporary loan to the Portland PB from a university in the UK.

"Okay," said Jess when they had all taken a seat and listened to the messages from CC on Sam's phone. "Colin knows the rough outline of what happened before, but let's just go through it all and make sure we are up to speed. Because this may affect Cove Beach as well as the city of Chinook and Duniway College. AJ, do you want to start?"

"Before we go forward," asked Colin, "why was this a Portland PB matter if the crimes were in Chinook?"

Jess took a moment to explain. The small town of Chinook retained just three full-time police officers on their force, and the college only hired security. "Given the scope of the first killings, the chief in Chinook asked for our help and resources. His team then provided support."

Colin nodded and wrote down a few notes. Jess then turned back to Sam.

"Right, and," said Colin, before Sam could start. "Oh, sorry, just one more thing." He then shifted in his body to face Sam. "How would you like to be addressed going forward? Anna, AJ, or Samantha? I think it might help us all keep things straight."

Sam paused for a moment. She almost laughed out loud. *Who am I?* she thought. *Does this guy know what he's asking?* She felt their eyes on her. *That is the question, isn't it? There's no time for an existential debate, Professor. Pick one!*

"Sam." She nodded her head. "Yes, Samantha McMican. The first killings are in the past, and that's where I want to keep them. This is my new life, and I'm not going to let this bastard take it from me."

They all nodded in agreement. Sam drew in a deep breath and began to tell her tale. For the next hour she and Jessica detailed the anonymous letters Anna Jean Morrill, her real name given at birth, started to receive five years ago. The letters, printed on heavy, pale yellow parchment paper and sealed with red wax, arrived before a murder happened.

Jess jumped in here to explain the seal, a stylized image of the capital letter "M," provided no link to the killer—too generic. She went on to add, the wax could be bought in any stationery store and online in a million different places.

The letters made mention of Sam's success as a professor and ranted about the ego she must have to think she could write a mystery novel. The quotes ran like, "those who can, do; those who can't, teach," and "just stay in the classroom where you belong." The more worrisome lines quoted her lectures. The police assumed the person had either been a student or sat in on the class, but to comb through the hundreds of students enrolled over the years became futile without anything specific to go on.

But the most horrific letter arrived first and talked about the victims being a family, just like the real-life family killed in England in 1811. Sam used the famous Ratcliffe Highway Murder case each term in her classes as an example of true crime sensationalism. A day later a makeshift "family" of three masters' students, who shared a house just off campus, were found dead. The investigation turned up nothing to tie the students to the English department, to any of Sam's courses, or her group of graduate students. Nothing about the three people explained why they'd been targeted.

The sign over the front door read, *The Addams Family.* One of the students hung it up as a joke. The old house stood as one of the last run-down, paint-peeling, Victorian houses in the town of Chinook. Could that link them as a family? Sam had been skeptical until she read the police report and looked at the crime scene photos. The images showed each of the students' heads bashed in and blood splattered on every surface of the living room. A long-handled maul lay on the rug beside one of the bodies.

The way they died connected to the Highway Murders, but unlike the gruesome slayings of 1811, the toxicology report showed drugs in their systems. The potent sedative had already killed two of them and left the third unconscious when the killer went to work bludgeoning the three students. The fourth victim made the case even more sensational. A brown and white spotted spaniel, found placed in the arms of his owner, died with his throat cut. The Ratcliffs' baby son, from the Highway Murders, had also been killed, and the small dog seemed to represent the murdered child.

The names and faces of the students now floated back up to the top of Sam's mind: Gina Lopez, Nathan Sutter, and Makala George. She remembered the nights she'd lain awake with their faces in front of her. Sometimes in the dark she screamed, *Why? Why? Why!* over and over into her empty bedroom as loud as she could and then sobbed herself to sleep.

After Jess and Sam recounted the killings from five years ago, Jess pulled on a pair of nitrile gloves and opened the evidence bag with the newest letter inside.

Hello, Anna Jean (or is it, Samantha?)

You thought you could just run away, that I wouldn't find you? Silly, silly girl. Of course, this isn't over. You've reinvented yourself. That's not part of the plan. There will be retribution for trying to escape me. This time, perhaps, the victims won't be strangers. That would make the game much more fun, wouldn't it? Maybe this time you will recognize the faces staring up at you with their pupils forever set. Maybe this time I'll play a bit fairer. You were so in the dark before. Not this time. I've left lots of clues. Fancy yourself a sleuth? Let's see if you're smart enough to figure it out.

Deadly Yours

"You can see why I'm so worried about CC," said Sam.

"It may not be just people from your college days," Jessica said. "If this person found you in Cove Beach—knows your alias—then we can assume they are watching you and anyone you may be close to there."

Marlene reached across the table with her pen and turned the letter around to read it again. "Not necessarily."

"What do you mean?" asked Colin.

Marlene looked up to see both Jessica and Colin's look of surprise.

"Cove Beach doesn't have home mail delivery, only post-office boxes."

When they both looked confused, Marlene said, "We are too small. There's no mail carrier going door to door. Everyone goes to the post office to pick up all mail, not just packages."

Sam smiled at the confused faces of the two investigators. "It's a small-town thing."

Jessica shook her head and chuckled. "You really do live in the boonies, don't you? So, what you are saying is that the killer may not know where Sam actually lives in town?"

Marlene and Samantha both nodded.

"Well, there's a small blessing," said Jess and then to Colin, "Anything you can make of this letter?"

"Right, umm, educated, I'd say intelligent. Calligraphy is a preset printer font, like before, so no handwriting clues there. Could be male or female. Statistics would lean toward white male. Stable family life."

Sam stared down at the letter for a moment and then got up to walk around the room. She just couldn't hold still. *It's all beginning again. What if a friend dies this time?* The thoughts made her brain hurt. Then a buzz started to fill her ears, just like in *The Chronicle* office the day before. She fought to contain the nausea. She would not faint here in a room filled with cops. She wouldn't let anyone think of her as weak or fragile.

Samantha, while never one to be accused of being delicate, fainted when stress overwhelmed her. It started when she fell off the swing in her backyard at four years old. A doctor explained it as her fight or flight response kicking in when she felt under attack or a sudden, intense fear. The doctor even went on to say, "Shows you are still in touch with your cavewoman reflexes for survival." Sam didn't find that funny, nor did she see how falling to the ground in front of a charging, wild beast would be to her advantage, unless playing dead worked as a strategy.

Sam excused herself to get a glass of water and left the conference room. As she opened the door and walked out into a sea of desks, a low roar of activity confronted her. Phones rang, elevator doors opened and closed, and cops shouted into phones. Off to Sam's right stood a water cooler and coffee station. She gulped down the first cold cup, refilled it, and then leaned against the counter.

A couple of officers looked up when she came out of the conference room, but with one glance, they lost interest. She caught a reflection of herself in the glass windows and understood why she no longer turned heads. *I'm so thin. When did that happen?*

She'd always been chubby. A chubby kid and a chubby adult with a life-long dream to be skinny. But now as she stared at her gaunt face in the glass, she knew she didn't want this. The weight loss from pain and grief, even though she had begun to gain some of it back in the past year, made her face look wrong. She looked old. Her hair, left to go gray after years of coloring it a dark, auburn brown, made it hard for her to recognize her own reflection. This unnerved her the most. She made so many changes to stay safe, but did those changes change her? *Have I lost myself?*

Just past the coffee station stood a large whiteboard. A young, tall officer paced in front of it as he made notes and pinned up photos. Sam's eyes drifted around the board. A photo of a sea chest caught her attention. Her head spun to the next picture which showed the same chest with a body inside. The note written alongside the image read, "killed by a sharp weapon—run through trunk into body." Her eyes scanned the top of the board and then stopped on the photo and the words written below—Victim Robert Brignone.

Samantha shoved herself away from the counter, then turned and ran back into the conference room. She wrenched the door wide open, raced inside, and slammed it shut. The three investigators huddled around the letter on the table stared up in alarm.

"Was that trunk found in a museum?" Sam demanded.

Jessica's face looked confused. "What trunk?"

"The body in the trunk!" Sam shouted and pointed

to the room behind her. "On the whiteboard. Was it found in a museum?"

Jessica squinted through the window to the squad room, and then her eyes darted back to Sam. *Shit! She's seen the incident board.* Jessica paused for a moment. Even though it contained details of an unrelated crime scene, she didn't want to discuss an ongoing case with a civilian.

Before Jess could respond, Colin stood up. "No, not in a museum exactly, but..." *There*, he thought as his voice trailed off, *a spark of recognition in her eyes behind the fear.*

The pitch of her voice rose. She turned toward Colin. "Then...a-a-a party? Was there a party in the room with the ch-ch-ch-chest?"

Jess and Marlene stared at her stunned. Colin answered again. "Yes." He walked over toward the door. "He was found in an old sea trunk two days after a party at his home."

Sam's next words came out as a whisper. "It's the killer."

Her hands shook as she reached out and grabbed hold of the closest chair. She stumbled into it so hard it began to roll away from her before she could sit down in the seat. In one fluid movement, Colin caught the back of the chair with his left hand and Sam's upper arm with his right. He then steadied the chair and sat her squarely in the seat. He reached out and pulled a nearby chair close to hers. Sam held her head in her hands. Colin sat down beside her.

In a soft voice, he asked, "Sam?"

Silence.

"Samantha," he said, with more force as he placed

his hand on her arm. "Please. Look at me."

Sam raised her head and looked into his green eyes. The scent of fresh cedar and bergamot wafted over her as Colin leaned in. It reminded her of walks in the woods and Earl Grey tea.

"What did you see? Tell me what you think happened."

Sam stared for another moment at those kind eyes and then went on to describe the murder details, the chest, the stabbing, all of it. When she finished, she put her head back in her hands and waited.

They all sat there in silence for a few minutes, and then the hammer came down. Jessica exploded. She stood over Sam with her arms folded across her chest. Her eyes flashed fire.

"Okay, would you care to explain how the fuck you know about this murder, which we only got called to yesterday morning! Only his name has been released. The press don't even have all the details yet."

"Because you taught this case to your students, didn't you?" Colin asked Sam. As his eyes took in her pale face, the back of his neck prickled like it had done at the crime scene.

Sam stared again into Colin's eyes. The muscles in her face and shoulders began to relax. "You see it too."

"I think so, but you will need to fill in the blanks for me."

Marlene jumped in. "Stop! Roll it back! Could you two Poindexters explain what in the hell is going on? Please! For Christ's sake!"

"Yes!" said Jess as her voice rose in volume and pitch. "And right now!"

"I won't bore you with all the background," said

Sam, "but let's just say that in detective literature there is an Agatha Christie novel where the victim hides in a chest to catch his wife cheating during a party and is then run through with a sword by the killer. I thought at first it might have been a reenactment of the P.D. James novel, *The Murder Room*. That's why I asked if the chest was found in a museum.

"In the Christie novel, the killer talked the husband into hiding in the chest. It was printed under different titles over the decades, but the most well-known is, *The Mystery of the Spanish Chest*. It can't be a coincidence."

"Don't rule out *The Murder Room* just yet," said Colin. He visualized the crime scene in his mind. "The body was found in a study that could have been taken for a museum. It was packed with antiques."

Sam's thoughts went to the photos on the board of the room and the body. Then with a slow nod of her head, she said, "Oh, so it could be PD James. But in the James novel the victim was shot before going into the trunk."

"Hmm, well, that would depend on how accurate the killer is trying to be with the murders," said Colin.

Jessica looked ready to have a stroke. "So, if this crazy theory you have is right, there's a well-read murderer out there killing people for sport? Or," she said, as a nerve in her right eye twitched, "is he hoping to become some sort of real-life literary sensation?"

With no answer to that question, Sam sat back in her chair and knew the moment had come. She had not only seen Bob's study before in photographs, but in person. She stood in that very room seven years ago for a party.

"And one more thing, and you're not going to like it." Sam took no pleasure in telling the detectives this bit of news. "I know—knew—Bob Brignone."

Chapter 7

August 21 – Police Bureau, Portland, OR

"What!" Jess and Marlene cried out at once, as Colin's head swung up to look at Samantha.

"Yes." Sam stared at the surface of the conference table. She couldn't bring herself to make eye contact with any of them.

"Okay." With an impatient toss, Jess threw her ponytail over her shoulder and walked toward the door. She called out to the young officer by the whiteboard. "Calhoun, could you please come in here and bring your notebook."

Jacob sat down and held up his phone.

"Yea, yea, whatever you take notes on," said Jess as she waved him into a seat. She then nodded to Sam. "Let's hear it. How are you connected to Robert Brignone?"

Sam hesitated. It amazed and intimidated her to see how Jess commanded her team. When they first met, Jessica had been the young number two taking orders from a well-worn, senior cop, who Sam found to be a bit of a dick. But now Jess stood there in complete control.

"It was about fifteen years ago. I had just been hired at Duniway College in Chinook to be a teaching assistant while working on my PhD. Bob, a woman named Alicia Alvarez, one named Priscilla Greene, and me, we all shared a cramped office space in the English department.

"Bob left first because he was the closest to finishing his doctorate in communications. He had been a reporter before Duniway but decided he wanted to add a few more letters to the back of his name. You know, he had the BS but wanted the MS and PhD to go with it. Then he went back to newspapers and worked his way up to management until, as you know, he became the editor of the *Northwest News Tribune*.

"Alicia was next, but she stayed in academia. She accepted a professorship somewhere back east. Or—" Sam paused to think for a minute. "—did she end up in the Midwest? I can't really remember. I didn't stay in touch with her. But Bob would sometimes come in and give a guest lecture for me when we got to the section of the course discussing the role of the media in true crime and scandal. That kind of thing."

Jess flipped through the old case notes. "Yes, we know Greene. She's the one we've been in contact with in trying to locate Cornelia. She's some sort of editor? At Upton Press?" She looked up at Sam for confirmation.

"Yeah, CC's managing editor. Her main point person really, for getting anything edited, printed, and distributed once CC makes the decision to publish a submission."

"And that was all of you?" Jess asked.

"In that one office? Yes, but there were two other offices, each with four T.A.'s—teaching assistants. Some were from the English department, some from history, other communications, and a couple from anthropology. It's such a small college, they dropped you into any space they could find. If you want information about any of those"—Sam pointed at the file in Jessica's hand—"we'd have to go through all those old police reports from five years ago. I really can't remember very many of them now, sorry."

"That's not a problem. Tell me more about—"

"Oh, no wait," Sam cut in. "I remember someone else. A manager...yes...hmm...what was his name...Paul?...Nelson?" She paused and thought back to those college days. "No, Paul Neilson. That's right! One of the main office administrators. Staff not faculty. He coordinated our office spaces, class schedules, our computer accounts, that kind of thing, for all the PhD candidates at Duniway. Paul was sort of our 'go-to' guy when we needed something. But he also stepped in if anyone was slacking on their office hours, student follow-up, you know the drill."

Sam looked over at Jessica's notes. "I'm sure you talked with him during the first killings."

Jess nodded. "I'll be looking at the file notes over the weekend. But let's finish up your information about Bob."

Sam went on to tell them what she remembered about the dead editor. He came from the old school of journalism, where facts and sources held a sacred place in the craft. When he filled in for a professor, word spread across the department and the classroom would be packed with students eager to hear his lecture. Because of his years in the trenches at large papers, Bob had a story for everything.

But his personal love for the Columbia River bar led to the collections of antiques. He couldn't resist memorabilia from the time when the Columbia River held the title of *the* trade route for goods up and down the river, from Seattle to San Francisco and back again. In the late 1800s the guild of Columbia River Bar Pilots, led by well-known Captain George Flavel, ran the city with an iron fist, and Bob collected all he could from that era. His fascination with these pilots who steered each large ship across the treacherous river bar to safe mooring in Astoria as they still do today, bordered on obsession.

"Bob could really make your eyes glaze over when he got to talking about Flavel and the river," Sam said with a sad smile. Everyone sat in silence for a few moments.

"And you say you've been in his home by the Japanese Gardens?" Colin asked. Sam felt his gaze on her like a specimen in a jar, all wide-eyed and clinical. An irritation rose inside her like smoke above a campfire ready to fill your lungs and burn your eyes.

"Yes." She responded in a blunt way her mother would have called rude, but her body ached from the restless night, and exhaustion pulled her muscles down like weights. She just wanted it all to be over. "He would normally host a get-together at his house in the summer."

"How does he identify? Gay? Bi? Queer? Do you know?" asked Jessica.

Sam sat there bewildered. "I have no idea. We weren't that kind of close."

"But he invited you to his annual party."

"That's really because of his guest lecturing. It kept us in touch. I'm sure it was just a courtesy on his part."

After another twenty minutes of questions, Jess

turned to Colin and Marlene. "Is there anything either one of you would like to know?"

Marlene looked at her own notes and said, "Back to this Priscilla and Alicia—"

Just then Jessica's phone rang. "Hold that thought," she said as she pulled it out of her pocket and looked down. "I need to take this."

She answered the call and stepped out of the conference room. The door shut behind her with a loud click. After several minutes on the phone, Jess returned and put her hand on the back of the young officer's chair. She looked first at Colin and then down at Jacob.

"Colin? Calhoun? Can I see you two outside for a minute? Thank you." She then turned to Sam and Marlene. "We'll be back. There's just something we need to discuss."

Both men gave each other an inquisitive look but said nothing. Then Sam noticed a change in all three of the detectives. Their faces went blank, and they each squared their shoulders. Jacob pocketed his phone, stood up, nodded to his boss, and left the room. Colin rose from his seat without a word and avoided eye contact with Sam and Marlene.

Through the conference room window, Sam could see the three of them huddled together. Jacob stood off to one side taking notes as he listened to the other two. After Jessica spoke the first few words, Colin's eyes flickered just for a moment toward Samantha, and then he shifted his body so she couldn't see his face.

"This can't be good," Sam began and then stopped when she turned back to Marlene. Her face looked blank just like the others, with her back rigid. She stared at the window.

"No," said Marlene. Then her head snapped up as Jessica gave Jacob some sort of order. The young man's face became like stone, his body stiffened, and with a quick nod of his head, he left the group. Jess now turned back to the window and locked eyes with Marlene. As Jess came back into the room, Marlene reached out and put a hand on Samantha's forearm. In a soft voice, she said, "Not good."

Chapter 8

August 21 – Pearl District, Portland, OR

A figure, dressed in a high-performance, black hoodie and matching running pants, stood behind the police line in front of a glistening high-rise. Positioned along the Willamette River in the popular and trendy Pearl District, stood Portland's—if the brochures could be believed—premiere condo building, The Apex.

Bodies jostled one another for a good position up front as more and more gawkers gathered. Rumors flew through the air like heat-seeking missiles. As the figure slipped through the crowd, they heard snippets of conversations: "What'd you think? Some local TV celeb took a kitchen knife to a lover in the shower or something?" and then, "Oo, maybe an obsessed fan knifed the celeb in the lobby," all followed by echoes of laughter and taunts. The city's reputation as a hotbed of protests and crime in the last few years made it anyone's guess. The speculation brought giddy reporters from all the major media outlets, along with a sea of amateur bloggers and influencers to the Pearl.

Photographers snapped photos in quick succession. Then, as if given a silent signal, the TV cameras all swung to the left. The bystanders' heads turned, and in unison they pushed forward. From a side street, a white van appeared with the city police logo painted on the side. It drove up over the curb and parked close by the front door. As the forensic team began to unload their gear from the back of the van, a man in a well-tailored navy suit and crisp white shirt with Italian leather shoes stomped forward from the glass turnstile door. The man waved his arms and pointed at the driver and then at the street. No one in the crowd could hear what he said, but the scowl on his face left no doubt as to his thoughts on the police invasion of the sidewalk and the lobby.

As all eyes focused on the angry suited man and the police officer who stepped up to take the brunt of his fury, no one noticed the dark-clothed figure as it left the crowd and began a slow, steady jog around the edge of the condos. They entered the Greenway Trail along the river and tugged the strings of the sweatshirt hood snug to their head. A satisfied smile broadened across the jogger's face, and a thought came to mind. *I think it's time for another letter.*

****

August 21 – Police Bureau, Portland, OR

"What happened!" Samantha cried out. Her brain raced and heart pounded. She didn't know how long she could hold it all together.

"I thought she was being picked up at the airport!" Sam shouted as she paced back and forth across the room. A ball of fury rose inside her chest. She stopped in the middle of the room and bellowed, "What the *fuck* happened!"

She didn't feel faint. No. She wanted to punch one of them in the face.

It had been about two hours since Jessica walked back into the conference room and told Sam a body had been found in her friend's apartment. Jess and

Marlene's voices stayed low and steady as they took the next few minutes and calmed Sam down. Jess explained how Cornelia caught an earlier flight from Chicago this morning instead of sticking to her original ticket—no idea why. She didn't call the station or contact Jessica with the cell number she gave her. When CC did not get off the plane at eleven forty-five a.m., like the patrol officers expected, they confirmed her earlier Alaska Airlines' flight and radioed another patrol to check her condo.

The four investigators stood together and discussed what to do next.

Marlene said, "I'll start working on her security detail once Sam and I get back to Cove Beach this afterno—"

"Like hell I'm going back." Sam cut her off. "I'm going to CC's."

All four of them turned to stare at her. Jessica shook her head.

Before they could argue, Sam said, "Look, I'm the close friend or relative you need to identify the body, right? And as for losing my ride back to Cove Beach? I'm certainly smart enough and capable enough to book a hotel room for the night and find my way home tomorrow, for Christ's sake."

After a heated debate, Sam now found herself in the hallway outside Cornelia's condo. With no more bravado left, she wrapped her arms tightly around her waist and pressed her back into the wall. Her head hung down as she swallowed her tears. The police officer assigned to stay with her looked twelve. With notebook in hand, she kept her focus on Sam and the apartment. The young officer's head swung around every time the door opened.

Sam pressed the skin between her eyebrows with her thumb to try and stop the pain. As it eased, her mind began to wander. *A body? In the apartment? Is it CC? Please let it not be CC. Oh, God, no. This can't be happening.*

Sam raised her head to see the officers and crime scene people, dressed from head to toe in white coveralls and surgical gloves, come and go. Then a woman's voice said, "Thank you, officer." Sam started as Jessica appeared at her side. "That won't be necessary." Jessica gave the officer a smile and nod. "We have Ms. McMican's details."

The officer relaxed her stance, nodded over Sam's left shoulder. "Yes, ma'am."

She then walked to the end of the hall by the elevators. Jess placed a hand on Sam's back. "Let's sit down for a minute."

Sam nodded and followed Jessica to the other end of the hall. They sat down together on the plush sofa placed against the wall. In the next ten minutes, Sam learned what a part of her brain already knew. The body of her good friend lay dead a few feet away. In the last four to six hours, Cornelia Cowan's heart stopped beating.

As Jess finished, Sam put her head between her knees. The sudden loss of her anger created a vacuum, and despair rushed in to fill the space. She took long, deep breaths in through her nose and exhaled out through her mouth. She stared between her feet at the black-and-white marble floor, polished to a high sheen. She tried her best not to throw up all over it.

With her full concentration now on the intricate

designs in the marble, she attempted to focus and hold herself together. *I will not faint twice in two days!*

Instead, her mind drifted off into nothingness as it conjured up ludicrous things.

...the marble is so white...so is Jessica's shirt...so white against her black pants and her dark skin...how does she not spill on that shirt?...the black streaks on the floor are so intricate ...did the black get into the white of the marble by geologic intrusion?...how many millions of years old do you think this marble is?...oh, God, I'm so nauseous...

"AJ? Sorry, Sam?"

Samantha again flinched at the sound of Jessica's voice. *God, don't be such a tweaker. Calm down before you get the yips.* She cleared her mind and glanced up. "Sorry, Jess. What were you saying?"

"Do you feel up to giving me a few more details about Cornelia? I know this is the worst time, but—"

"Of course, but I'm going to keep my head down while we talk."

Jess rattled off her questions. Sam answered.

Yes, we had been friends for years

No, we hadn't spoken recently

Her message was the first I'd heard from her in probably a year

Yes, I knew she was gay

No, we weren't lovers

No, we never really talked about who she dated, just the occasional note about someone new, or an excited text when she had dumped the latest

No, she hadn't talked about anyone recently

No fights, and nothing at work as far as I knew but CC probably wouldn't have told me anyway

"I'm thinking we should get you outta here." Jess closed her notebook with a snap. "This is the last place you need to be."

Sam's head cleared, but her brain still seemed slow to comprehend it all. She knew she needed to sound and act like a professional, even if she didn't feel it, and not a babbling idiot. So, she sat up straighter and turned her full attention to Jessica. "No, you're going to need me to look at the crime scene."

"No." Jessica put her hands up and shook her head. "There's no way you are going in there, not in this state." As Sam began to protest, she said, "Not now."

"I think she should see it," said Colin. Both women swung their heads up in unison. Neither one of them heard him approach.

Jessica bolted out of her seat. "No, Colin. This isn't the right time—"

"I'll do it," Sam cut her off. "I just need a minute." She put her head back between her knees and took a few more long, deep breaths.

Jess put her hand on Sam's back and gave Colin a look that told him just how far over the line he had stepped. If not for the fact he didn't technically work for her, she would have fired him on the spot. Colin stood in the hallway unconcerned.

After one more pointed look, Jessica pulled her eyes away. "Sam, we don't need you to look right now. In a few hours maybe you—"

Before Sam could offer up another protest, a faint bell sounded at the other end of the hall as the elevator settled itself in place. The young female officer marched toward the three of them. She spoke into the radio attached to her shoulder. "Give me a minute to check with Detective Noguchi."

"What is it?" asked Jess.

"There's someone named," the officer said as she looked down at her notes, "Priscilla Greene? In the lobby asking to come up. Says she works for the deceased...I mean..." The officer stopped and looked wide-eyed at Sam's bent-over form as she caught her mistake, and her face flushed. The officer's gaze darted back to her notebook, and then, with more care, she said, "Sorry. She works for the woman in the apartment. Says she's just driven up from Chinook? When she couldn't reach—" The officer paused again to look at her notes. "—Cornelia Cowan?"

Jess turned to Sam and asked, "This is the Greene I've been talking to at Upton? Also, from your Duniway days? You shared an office, right?"

"Right. Now CC's managing editor."

Jessica nodded, walked over, and asked the officer to bring Priscilla up but to hold her at the elevators. Sam called out, her head still down between her legs. "Jess...wait!"

Startled, both she and Colin spun around to face Samantha. With care, so she didn't get sick, Sam raised her head. "Not to state the obvious but she's going to know me as AJ. What do I say when all of you call me Samantha?"

Jess raised her hand to stop the officer from radioing downstairs and then stood for a moment. "I think it's going to be tricky keeping your new alias separate from your past identity. What do you think, Colin?"

"Do you think it's even possible to go back to AJ Morrill?" asked Sam, before Colin could answer.

"No," Colin said without hesitation. "I think you're buggered if you try to juggle them both and for very little result. This current letter came addressed to your alias. Clearly the killer knows, so keeping it from everyone else is probably an immense waste of time."

Jess nodded. "I agree."

Sam sighed and sat up taller. "Me too, but thanks for trying to give me an out. I'm just going to have to explain the whole damn fuck-up to everybody."

"Not exactly," said Colin to Jess not Samantha. The two looked at each other. "You agree?" Jess nodded her head.

Colin turned back to Sam. "We don't want you interacting with anyone from the past if we can avoid it." Sam looked confused. He went on. "You need to stay as far away from this and the press as you can."

Jessica turned to the officer eager for instructions. "Please have them hold Ms. Greene in the lobby and tell her someone will be down to talk with her shortly." The officer nodded and walked down the hall as she spoke into her radio.

"Are you sure about that?" Sam asked as she pushed herself off the sofa. She did her best to stand up as straight as she could. "Don't you want to see how these potential suspects react to me?"

Both Colin and Jess gave each other a pointed look, and then Colin said in a soft voice, "This isn't a mystery novel. We aren't going to use you as bait and hope the killer tries to attack you here in the hallway."

While before his voice calmed her, this sound grated on Sam's nerves. She knew a teacher's voice when she heard it. She had used it enough with her own students. *I'm not playing that game*, she thought. Sam put her hands on her hips and squared her shoulders.

"Well, that's a little short-sighted, don't you think? Mystery novel or not, this killer wants me to suffer by making me the center of these killings. Why not put a few of these people from my past in the hot seat and crank up the heat?"

Jessica stepped between the two of them. "Sam, I know this isn't easy for you, but you need to see how right now, your safety is our top priority. You are the key to finding this bastard. You stay alive, and we might just catch him."

Sam's face flushed, and she felt sweat forming under her armpits and behind her knees. *No,* she thought, *not a damn hot flash! Not now! Ignore it and stand your ground.*

"But you're going to need me to look at this scene." What started as a question in her mind became a command as Sam spoke the words. She would not be taken away so easily without a fight. Five years ago, she would have let them push her around—not today. She would not run. She had reached the limit of being told what to do.

Jess bit down on her lower lip and looked over at Colin who nodded in agreement. "Yes, we would like you to see the scene." She then parceled out her next words. "But listen to me. If you feel like you're going to drop, or more importantly vomit, you need to let us get you out of there. You could contaminate the crime scene."

Sam took a long, deep breath. "Got it."

As they walked down the hall to Cornelia's door, Sam steeled herself against what she might confront in the apartment and concentrated only on the details:

things out of place, smells, temperature, broken furniture, and the like. She learned this reporter's trick from Mike when they covered their one and only murder in Cove Beach a few months after she started at the paper.

"Just look at the details. Don't get pulled in by the horror of it," Mike had said. "Then you can see the big picture and write an honest account. What you feel has no place in journalism, no place in your story."

The open concept of CC's condo allowed Sam to see straight through the living and dining area to the corner of the kitchen island. Bright morning light poured in through the bank of large windows that lined the east wall. Through the glass shone the Willamette River. More than a decade ago, the publisher had taken her New York money and bought a condo in The Apex, a large condo building right on the waterfront in the Pearl. She said, "If I'm going to live at the fucking ends of the earth, I'm not going to give up comfort or style."

CC's apartment looked and felt the same as her office: cold, orderly, and filled with sleek mid-century modern furniture and art. Sam always teased CC about there not being one comfortable place to sit in the whole condo. She tried to convince her friend to add just one old beat-up leather chair. CC would shake her head and call Sam an uncultured peasant.

In the hallway outside the apartment, all three of them pulled covers over their shoes. Colin walked through the door first, and Sam started to follow. Before she could cross the threshold, Jessica stepped in front of her and held out a small blue jar. "Here, put a little dab under your nose before you go in."

As she took the container from Jess, she noticed

the words Vick's VapoRub on the label. Sam looked up confused.

"It'll help keep you steady when you see the body."

Sam's look changed to skepticism.

"No, really, it works. It's what the MEs use. Trust me."

Sam opened the blue jar and dipped her pinky finger into the salve. She didn't see how this would make a difference but went ahead and put a smear under each nostril. The menthol smell went straight to the top of her nose. Her sinuses widened. Memories of her mother rubbing Vicks on her chest and back flashed into her head. *Maybe that's how it works*, she thought. *It makes you feel safe.*

As Sam entered the apartment, she could see Cornelia's body being lifted out of a stainless-steel dining room chair. The position of the body stopped Sam in place. CC's body leaned over the chair as if all her muscles seized at once. Her upper body draped at an awkward angle over the chair arm, and her forearms stayed bent. As the MEs moved the chair away from the table, her body shifted sideways. Her arms didn't fall to her sides. Sam stepped up to the table and looked at her friend's face. Horrific. Her brain could think of no other word. Cornelia Cowan was gone, replaced by a contorted figure. A grotesque.

"Yes," said Sam, "that's her. Cornelia."

Sam averted her eyes and stepped out of the way as one of the examiners pushed a gurney toward the body. A cold breeze touched her skin. She wrapped her arms around her rib cage to stop from shivering. She glanced up to see one of the windows cracked open.

She started to speak, but as she tried to form the words, her mouth felt like chalk. She coughed to clear her throat. "Can I know the time of death?"

Jess looked over at the forensic team and directed her gaze to a woman crouched down on the floor under the dining room table. She gave the lead medical examiner for the case, Julie Carl, a nod.

"Given the liver temperature, time of death should be no more than six hours ago," said Carl as she moved around a table leg to stand up.

That can't be right, thought Sam. Past research projects for several mystery writers gave her a basic understanding of forensics. Her mind went back to what she knew about Cornelia's flight. *If CC had definitely landed around ten this morning and it's now just after three, there hasn't been enough time for her friend's body to be in full rigor.*

In the next moment ME Carl confirmed her suspicions. "But if that temp is right, then this rigor mortis is doing something bizarre." Carl shook her head. "I'll gather more information and get back to you after the autopsy."

"I don't want to look again," said Sam. She turned away from the gurney as another examiner zipped the black bag closed. She would never admit it to anyone in this room, but she now regretted her demand to enter the apartment. The image of her friend's mouth fixed in a grimace with her lips parted and her teeth set tightly together now floated before her. "Do you think CC's face contorted due to this rigor?"

"Yes," said the thirty-three-year-old forensic specialist without emotion. She waved her hand to her team, and the body continued to be moved out of the apartment. Carl then turned her attention back to the carpet. As the ME crouched down, Sam could just see her close-clipped, shining black hair through the fine mesh of the pale-yellow fibers of the medical hood.

Sam moved to the kitchen. "Were there any cards found?"

"Cards?" asked Colin. His neck prickled.

"Playing cards." Sam now stood by the sink.

Jess turned toward the crime scene staff and asked about cards.

"I just bagged them," said one of the examiners. He held up the evidence bag. "Seven cards." He turned them over in his hands. "Looks like from a standard deck." Sam nodded.

Careful not to touch any surface, she crouched down to get a closer look at the basin. Droplets of water clung to the strainer. She turned her head to look at the underside of the faucet. No drips.

Sam's eyes then landed on two tiny drops of red candle wax on the kitchen counter. She pivoted to face the open space of the condo. A scan of the room confirmed what she already knew. CC didn't have a single candle anywhere. Her gaze drifted to the dining room table. There sat a small candle holder with traces of red wax burned down to the rim. Sam considered this for a moment. *The VapoRub must have masked the smell of a burning wick.*

"Was music playing when you came into the condo?" she asked as she moved away from the kitchen. "Really upbeat stuff? Party music? Or laughter?"

Silence.

Sam stopped and looked up to see all eyes on her.

Jessica stood, once again, with her arms crossed in front of her. Colin looked bewildered as he stood with his hands on his hips. The rest of the officers just stared.

Jess let out a sigh and shook her head. "Son of a bitch. Laughter, playing on her laptop, yes. How in the hell did you know that?"

"Let me see if I can answer that one," said Colin. He looked at Sam for encouragement.

She just opened her hands, palms up, and shrugged.

"You asked about playing cards?" He walked over and picked up the evidence bag with the cards.

Sam nodded.

"Then the music? But you asked about laughter specifically?"

She nodded again.

"It's the way your friend's body was found, correct?"

"Yes, ME Carl said the rigor looks wrong for the time of death, but I think it might be right for…" Sam's voice trailed off.

"Quite!"

"And the candle wax." Sam pointed to the kitchen counter. "Which is why, I'm guessing, the window is open? There was a weird smell when you came into the room?"

Colin's eyes widened. "Yes." The solution twigged. "Shall I say it, or shall you?"

Sam shrugged her shoulders again. "If you think you have it, go for it."

"Jessica, this time it's Sherlock Holmes." He turned back to Sam. "Am I correct?"

A profound sadness pulled on her like a weighted blanket. "Yes, I think so. *The Adventure of the Devil's Foot.*"

Chapter 9

August 21 – West Slope Suburb, Portland, OR

"Well, it's a hell of a mess," said Jess as she handed around glasses and the whiskey bottle for everyone to take what they wanted. Then she flopped down on the well-worn sofa next to Sam. The sing-song sound of "*I'm a powerful dump truck*" rang out from the couch as her rear end landed on the cushion. She leaned on to Sam for a moment and reached around to pull forth a colorful little toy. With a snort, she turned off the switch to the little truck and tossed it into a basket by the red-brick fireplace and nestled back down. "There are land mines everywhere in this damn house," Jess said.

"You wouldn't have it any other way," said a deep voice in the kitchen.

Around the corner walked a tall man with a plate of chocolate chip cookies in his hands. "You love the chaos, and you know it. Oh, and hey, watch the language," he said as he nodded his head over his shoulder in the direction of the hallway. "You know they aren't asleep yet, only faking."

Jessica gave her husband a look of feigned shock at the reprimand. She put her hand to her heart and bowed her head. "Yes, dearest."

She then spread her arms wide and swept them in a

big arc. "I do love the two little blessings in the next room, but look at the mess they leave—everywhere. But"—she turned to Sam and Colin—"the mess I started to talk about was the case, not the acres of toys, and hair clips, and clothes all over the place."

Danny Cooper, a medical examiner for the Portland PB, put the plate down on the coffee table. He waved everyone to help themselves as he pushed aside the now empty Thai food take-out containers. "Sorry I wasn't there today. It sounded fascinating. But Carl is good. She'll get the job done. Oh...*shit!* Sorry, Samantha. I forgot."

Danny took the call that morning and dispatched Julie Carl instead of taking the case himself. The department policies didn't allow spouses to work together unless no other ME could be found on duty at the time.

"Excuse me," said Jess, "did you not just tell me to watch *my* language?"

Danny stopped with his right hand outstretched over the plate of cookies and looked up at his wife. He then did what she had just done a moment before. He put his hand on his heart and bowed his head. The two grinned at each other.

Sam smiled at the secret language of couples. Without warning, her eyes misted. She ducked her head to dab the tear and locked eyes with Colin. His pointed stare set Sam's teeth on edge as her jaw worked back and forth. *What was he trying to figure out?* she wondered. She gave him a small smile which irritated her even more because of her incessant need to be polite before she turned back and said, "Not to worry, Danny, I'm getting used to it."

"We always talk shop after we get the girls down to bed. I wasn't thinking about a civilian in the room." He finished with a heart-melting smile.

She couldn't help but grin back. Sam found Daniel Cooper far too handsome for anyone's good. He stood as least six feet tall, just an inch or so taller than Jessica, with perfect dark skin. His broad shoulders reminded Samantha of another man from another lifetime. At only thirty-nine and on track to be the police bureau's top forensic specialist in a few short years, this guy had it all.

She sipped her whiskey and listened to the back and forth between Colin and Danny. The two men talked with excitement as they dissected the facets of the case. Danny's eyes lit up when they talked about the possible poisons that could have caused the unusual rigor. Colin stayed focused on the psychology of the killer's mind.

Jess rested her head on the back of the sofa and closed her eyes. She tried hard not to think about what might be coming next.

Sam's mind raced as it flashed up images from the past two days. When she left CC's apartment, she asked for a few minutes alone. She took the elevator down to the main floor and found an empty stall in the public restrooms in the lobby.

As she started to hang up her backpack on the door hook, the pen and small notebook she always carried with her dropped out of an exterior pocket. When she bent down to pick them up, the right ankle of the woman in the next stall caught her attention. She couldn't take her eyes off the woman's shoes.

Look at those heels! she thought. *Must be four*

inches at least. How does she stand let alone walk in those things? She and CC were cut from the same cloth. She roused herself and gave her head a shake. A*ll this insanity around and you focus on her shoes? You are losing it, my friend.*

In the next moment her mind drifted once again. *Socks go with shoes. What! For fuck's sake, pull yourself together!*

Now, as she sat on the soft couch in the Coopers' cozy living room, her body started to relax, and another bout of tears jabbed at her eyes. She needed to be alone.

Sam leaned over and whispered into Jessica's ear, "If it's all right with you, I'm going to go to bed. The whiskey just hit bottom, and I can barely hold my head up."

"Of course." Jessica reached out and squeezed Sam's hand. "Let me show you the way."

Down the hallway, Jess led Sam to their guest room. She had protested earlier when Jessica ruled against a hotel. She didn't want to take any chances with Sam's safety, or her own.

"Look," Jess said to Sam once they were back at the station, "this nutjob could be watching you right now, and do you know how easy it is to break into a hotel room? No! The other option is to put you up in one of the department's crappy safe houses, but then I would be the one to stay with you anyway. Taking you back to my place keeps you safe, and I get to be with my girls."

That speech left Sam no room to argue. As she slipped between the cool, cotton sheets, nestled down into the pillow-top mattress, and pulled the soft colorful quilt around her, she felt grateful Jessica had told her to "shut up and get in the car."

Chapter 10

August 22 – Portland, OR

The next morning, as Samantha called Judith, Cornelia's older sister in New York, a few miles away a gloved hand slid an envelope of yellow parchment emblazoned with a red wax seal into a blue mailbox. Serenity spread across the sender's face as the letter moved over the rollers and dropped with a thwack on top of the other parcels and envelopes. *She will have the letter tomorrow. Everything is working perfectly this time.*

Sam, oblivious to the threat ahead, talked with Judith about funeral arrangements and the family's Jewish traditions when it came to losing a loved one. Jessica explained CC's suspicious death when she talked with Judith the day before. While Cornelia's sister recoiled at the thought of an autopsy, she understood why it needed to be done. Judith knew evidence, as a path to justice, superseded religious requirements.

"Anna Jean?"

CC stayed true to her word over the years and never told her family about Sam's new identity.

"Judith!" Sam's voice broke, and tears formed in her eyes. "I'm so, so sorry about CC. I wanted to call you as soon as I saw…" Sam stopped before she said too much. No one else needed to hear about Cornelia's body. She checked herself and went on. "I realized I didn't have your number in my phone now that you don't have a place in the city anymore. And I had to wait for the police to let me look through CC's cell phone."

"Oh, AJ, I completely forgot to get it to you when we moved to Long Island permanently," said Judith, always gracious. "There was just so much to do this spring. But I finally stepped out of the dark ages and got a cell phone."

Sam smiled and remembered how CC moaned about her sister being the last holdout on the planet without a cell phone. She berated her for more than a decade to just "buck up and do it."

Samantha didn't need Judith's number—land or cell. They only knew each other through Cornelia and only met half a dozen times over the years when Judith made those rare trips to Portland. But true to form and good upbringing Judith made the excuse of forgetting to protect Sam's feelings. And, she also remembered, when Judith said Long Island, she meant The Hamptons!

"Hi ya, A-Jaxs," said a deep voice through the phone. "How ya holdin' up?"

"Oh, Jules." Sam wiped the wetness off her cell phone screen and put the phone back up to her ear. "You're there too. So good to hear your voice—your voices—both of you. So, so wish we could be talking in person."

Sam longed to talk with Judith and Jules face-to-face. Right now, she would be wrapped in a huge bear hug by them both. CC came off as this tough, savvy

New Yorker, but a contagious happiness engulfed her family and friends.

Judith and Jules Sohn just celebrated their fiftieth wedding anniversary in March. As CC told it, "They found each other in college and were stupid enough to get married." Cornelia could never imagine being with anyone for more than a few dates, let alone five decades.

After a few minutes of that small talk people make when things are too serious to plow into head on, Judith asked, "Why do you think CC called you?"

"I don't really know. She just said, 'I think I fucked up' and to call her as soon as I could. But, Judith, you need to know, she was scared." Sam added, "I didn't really understand until I stepped off the elevator yesterday afternoon and saw her apartment, but now it's making more sense."

After a long pause, Judith sighed and said, "I just can't think about all of that right now with what needs to be done for the service."

The resignation in Judith's voice made Sam's heart ache. Her sister, now labeled a body instead of a living human being, would never walk through the door again. Memories of this time in Sam's own life crashed through her thoughts. She thought back to the little black dress, the fixed sad smile on her face, and an endless line of well-wishers. Her head hurt as she recalled the horrible injustice of those two words, "making arrangements." *Whose brilliant idea was it for the bereaved to be expected to plan the equivalent of a stage show followed by a banquet?* she thought. *It was both cruel and exhausting.*

But no matter her own pain, Sam couldn't put her

grief for CC on par with CC's family. While being good friends, Sam and CC saw each other only a few times a year, and with her move to Cove Beach, not at all. She and CC shared fun not feelings and the reason why Samantha chose Cornelia as her confidant in the first place. Her no-nonsense, cut-the-crap attitude made her the one person who would always keep her secret and tell her the truth.

So, what did she say or do to make her call me panicked she had given away my location? And more importantly, to whom had she said it? Sam could only wonder.

The call finished with a promise to get in touch. Judith gave permission to let Sam into the apartment and look through whatever she thought might help with the investigation. She and Jules would work with Jessica to have Cornelia's body flown to New York. The burial would need to take place as soon as possible after the autopsy.

While Jessica went back to the Brignone house to finish the examination of the crime scene, Colin and Samantha arrived at The Apex. Sam asked the night before if she might be able to go through CC's condo, once the forensic team finished with the scene. Since they still needed to sort out Cornelia's papers and personal items, Colin offered to accompany Samantha to ensure the chain of evidence until Noguchi could meet them at the condo.

The same fresh-faced, uniformed female officer Sam met the day before stood guard at the condo door as she and Colin got off the elevator.

"Morning, sir, ma'am," said the officer as Colin showed his ID card.

Sam thought to herself, *Ma'am, hot flashes, and chin hair—the indignities never end.*

She expected to see CC's condo in the same state as when she left it the day before, but as she stepped into the open space, she couldn't stop a small gasp. Yesterday the jumble of people, furniture, and books seemed appropriate given the murdered body of her friend, but today she entered another world.

While the police didn't ransack the place, they didn't miss much in their search. The bookcases stood almost empty with books stacked on the floor. Cabinet doors in the kitchen hung open with dishes strewn across the countertops. Towels and linens poked out of half-opened drawers. When she peered across the condo through the open door to CC's bedroom, she saw the same mess.

Sam's eyes landed on a stack of family photographs on the floor by an open photo album. Sooty gray fingerprints covered images of smiling faces, the family's old station wagon, CC and Judith on their first day at school, and more. The magic dust revealed a hidden record of ghostly figures who came, went, and touched everything. A shiver ran up her arms as she surveyed the room. Every surface contained the powdery etchings of a life once lived.

Sam's sudden pause inside the doorway caused Colin to sidestep around her. He asked in the same soft voice from the day before, "Are you all right?"

His words pulled her eyes from the bookcase. Today, those low tones didn't cause the same annoyance as they did the night before. She smiled and said, "Don't panic. I'm not going to yell at everyone again."

Colin replied, unfazed, "Not to worry. You had every right to throw a wobbly yesterday. I'm surprised you didn't punch your hand through a wall."

"Marble." She pointed to the far side of the room. "Like the floors. Would have broken all my fingers." They both laughed.

Colin liked the sound of her laugh but shook his head, amazed she could still make jokes. "Seriously, your self-control through all of this has left me gobsmacked. Not sure if I could have stayed as calm."

"Just be glad you aren't in my head right now. It's like a horror film in there." She let out a long sigh, and then in a whisper she said, "The nightmares are coming back."

Colin stopped and looked again at this relative stranger in front of him. He felt gutted for what she must have gone through years before, and now for it all to start again must be unbearable. Her exhaustion showed in her almost colorless face and slumped shoulders. In just the few hours he had spent with her, Colin found her to be a lovely woman, and he could see the understated beauty of her features. A veil formed by stress and time worked hard to conceal her own natural joy.

"How do you even know where to start? I've never seen this kind of thing before, in person. Only in photos or," she went on a little embarrassed to admit, "on TV."

"Right, yes, it can be chilling the first time. Everything tossed about, print dust everywhere."

The two of them moved about the apartment in silence for the next hour or so. Samantha searched through books and files for any reason CC would have called her. Colin studied Cornelia's photos, letters, and keepsakes for anything that would tell him more about her life and possibly the killer.

On the far side of the couch, Sam came across the editor's leather briefcase on top of a stack of magazines with wispy fingerprints clustered around the handle. She reached out to open the case and then stopped.

Sam pointed to the clasp on the case and asked, "Is it okay if I…?"

Colin walked over to the couch. "Actually, you are going to have to wait until that gets boxed up and is back at headquarters. Sorry—"

"She can look at it. I'm here," said Jessica as she walked through the door. "Sam, you know what? Bring it over to the table, and we can all take a look."

Jessica reached with her gloved hand into the middle section of the shoulder briefcase and pulled out a stack of file folders. A corner of a newspaper stuck outside one of the folder's margins. When Jessica opened it, the front page of *The Chicago News Tribune* dated the twentieth of June sat on top.

Jessica slid the folder over to Sam and asked, "Do you want to start with this?"

As she lifted the file up to get a better look at the paper, an old clipping from the back fluttered to the floor. She picked it up and smiled when she read her own byline. A few years ago, Mike assigned her to cover a local murder case for *The Chronicle*. A state legislator found herself in a world of hurt when she played political games with the wrong "organized" Oregon family. While on vacation in Cove Beach that summer, the game came to a full stop when her body washed up in the estuary on North Beach.

Samantha played only a small part in the

investigation but worked with a couple of detectives from Salem. Mike gave her some wise advice when he encouraged her to play the role of ally instead of antagonist. He told her, "You have a choice. You can be an asshole and stand on the outside looking in, or you can show a little cooperation and be right in the middle of the action."

Sam smiled at the memory. When focused on a project or story, she preferred a bulldozer to a spoon full of sugar and adhered to the old saying, "well-behaved women rarely make history." But this time Mike's approach had been the right one. The police, surprised by her attitude, kept her in the loop as the investigation developed.

She also got to know Marlene and the other local cops in the Cove Beach Police Department and many of the emergency response volunteers who lived in town. This became her biggest asset going forward as a local reporter.

She sent the clipping to Cornelia in reaction to one of the last things CC said to her when she left Chinook. CC always thought she should disappear into a big city. "Easier to hide in a crowd," she said. She even offered to help her relocate to New York, and not waste away in some backwater beach town. "You can still have a life."

Sam noticed her old note paper-clipped to the article.

See, it's not all judging bake sales and flower shows here in the thriving metropolis of Cove Beach. A mafia hit no less! And yours truly in the thick of it.

For CC to be sentimental enough to save the article left Sam speechless. Sam remembered the hard-nosed editor's response to the clipping. "Oh, for Christ's sake, stop wasting away at that little local rag."

Sam put the old *Chronicle* article aside and began to scan *The Chicago News Tribune*. One showed a photo of a state politician who got his hand caught in the cookie jar, with a sex scandal to boot. Another reported on the political gridlock in D.C. The main piece above the fold showed a photo of a historical church leveled in Mexico City from a 6.8 earthquake.

Nothing seemed to be tied to Cornelia or her work. Sam sat and stared at the paper for a few moments. Her brain raced with questions. *Why keep a paper this old? And in a file folder? Why a Chicago paper?* Then another thought hit her. *Do I know enough about CC to even answer these questions?*

She knew there had to be something important somewhere in these files. CC wouldn't have kept all this old stuff for no good reason. *Look around this condo*, she thought. *Nothing extra. Not a thing out of place until the forensic team got ahold of it*. She flipped the paper over, and in the bottom half of the fold she saw a story about a death in Chicago's largest hospital.

The headline read, *Professor Killed While Prepped for Surgery*.

The investigation left the police to wonder how someone could have walked up to a victim on a surgical gurney, strangle them, and then walk away without being seen. Sam's thoughts slipped sideways, and her heart pounded in her ears.

Strangled on a gurney, thought Sam, as she tried to keep her breathing as slow as possible. She let her mind meander down this path. *The killer probably wasn't a member of the surgical team. They could have just shot something into the IV making it seem like heart failure from the stress of the operation. Wait a minute. I know this story.*

The article included a small black-and-white photo of a woman about fifty, in a dark suit jacket with brunette hair streaked white along her temples. It looked to be a studio shot, not a candid, with a caption reading Alicia Alvarez, Director of English Literature.

Sam dropped her head in her hands and exhaled a long breath out. "Son of a bitch!"

"What is it!" Jessica's head swung toward Sam as she looked up from the papers in front of her.

Colin looked up from reading over Jessica's shoulder and walked over to Samantha. He glanced down at the newspaper headline and then the back of Sam's head slumped in her hands. He leaned in and said close to her ear, "Samantha, let me take a look."

With care, he lifted her elbow off the paper and slid it over so he could read the article. As he let go, Sam just let her elbow drop back to the table.

For a few moments no one said a word. Colin and Jessica scanned the articles on the page to see what would have caused Samantha's extreme reaction. Colin's eyes darted across the page and stopped at the top of the second paragraph. He placed his finger under the victim's name and tapped the page. Jess's eyes went straight to Colin's index finger.

"Fuck me." Jessica exhaled.

As they read through the article, they learned that Alvarez taught at one of the large colleges in Chicago. She started twelve years ago and held the director's position for the last three. When they finished, Colin lifted the paper up to get a better look at the photo.

Out of the corner of her eye, Sam caught a flash of neon pink.

"Wait, there's something stuck to the side."

As Colin turned the paper, they all noticed a sticky note with the words *Ellery Queen?* written in pencil beside the name Alicia Alvarez.

"'That's it!" Sam shouted out loud.

She wrenched her backpack out from under the table and flopped it down on the top. To herself she said, "I need a piece of paper," as she opened the bag and drew out her pen and notebook.

"Ellery Queen, Ellery Queen," she mumbled to herself, "but which one was that? They wrote so many, and then there was the TV show."

She closed her eyes and took a few deep breaths to try to clear a path in her mind. After a long exhale, the Ellery Queen stories floated to the top. An old story of a woman strangled by the doctor's assistant as she prepped her for surgery flashed into Sam's head. But she couldn't capture the details. She didn't always include Queen in the required readings for The Art of Detection, so she needed to dig deep.

"Sam?" began Jessica.

Sam raised her hand and said, "Shh! I need a minute."

Jessica's eyes widened at the abrupt command, but she stayed silent.

Sam told herself, let go of all the traffic noises from the street below, the hum of the refrigerator, and the tick-tock of the clock on the mantel. *Who still has a ticking clock anymore? Stop that and concentrate!*

About a minute later she reached for her pen and jotted down every thought in her head before they slipped away:

> *Ellery Queen*
> *Waiting for surgery*
> *Strangled with tubing?*
> *Diabetic?*
> *Killer dressed in scrubs*
> *Never the first suspect, so not the doc*
> *Doc's assistant engaged to the doctor's nephew?*
> *Killed for inheritance*

"Jess?" Sam asked as she scribbled the last few thoughts down. "Would there be a way to find out if Alicia was a diabetic?" She then glanced up to find four eyes fixed on her.

"Diabetic? What in the world are you talking about?"

Colin stood there amazed. "It's another one, isn't it? An old mystery?"

Sam nodded. "American this time. CC was right. Ellery Queen's *The Dutch Shoe*."

Chapter 11

August 22 - Seaview, OR

"Oh my God! If this light doesn't change in the next three seconds, I'm going to scream!" cried a frenzied Vicki Mathews. She'd been parked at a red light for what seemed like a decade. A summer of nonstop tourists exacts a toll from the locals, and today Vicki'd had enough.

She would never have left Cove Beach to drive the ten miles north into Seaview on an August afternoon if her daughter hadn't called from Astoria in a panic. Due to a rear-end smashup between an RV and an old pickup truck on Hwy 101, Ellen couldn't get through on the Youngs Bay Bridge. She told her mom she had already waited twenty minutes and only moved fifty feet.

"Oh, Mom, you can't believe the traffic. The bridge was like a parking lot, and of course, once you're on it, there's like nowhere to get off. It's insane. Please, can you pick up Hazel from her swim lesson?"

Vicki hung up and grabbed her purse from behind the counter. She turned the bookstore over to Lisa Hoptowit, a local graduate student and her one and only employee, as she dodged customers and raced out the back door. Over her shoulder, Vicki called out and promised Lisa a bonus if she didn't quit before she got back.

Now back in Cove Beach, she turned right just off Sitka Street onto Third and glanced at the front of her shop on the corner. The outside of the building defied the laws of physics. The top level of the house teetered above a narrow ground floor, and from the street it appeared to be leaning to the left.

Vicki remembered the first time she stepped into the shop almost ten years ago. She found the smell of old books tucked into wooden shelves patinated with age along with bits and bobs crammed into every corner irresistible. She stood in a real bookstore, with wing-backed chairs and squishy sofas plunked here and there and fell in love on the spot.

Once in the driveway, she rammed the car into *Park*, jumped out of the driver's seat, and breathed a sigh of relief. She then went to the back of the car and helped her five-year-old granddaughter out of her car seat. Hazel wrapped her little arms around Vicki's neck and whispered in her ear, "I like riding home with you, Granny. You're fun."

Vicki smiled and took her granddaughter's hand as they walked in through the back door of the store.

Vicki looked toward the edge of the old bar that served as her front counter. This remnant of the house's short-lived incarnation as a pub (circa 1940) came from the salvaged wooden panels found in the captain's quarters of an old shipwreck in Astoria. The ornate, milky mirror no longer hung behind the counter. Instead, floor-to-ceiling bookshelves now stood rooted in its place, but the bar and its old beer taps remained. Vicki could see both tills had already been closed out and the store locked up.

She called out. "Lisa, are you still here?"

"Nope," a voice answered from the coffee counter at the back of the store. "No Lisa. Just me."

Vicki stopped in the middle of the store. "Kimberly Wallis! What in the world are you doing here already?" Her eyes glanced toward the old grandfather clock to double-check the time.

A tall, slender, bronze-skinned woman in a crisp, white sundress stepped out from behind the counter and wrapped her arms around one of her dearest friends and book clubber.

Kim squeezed Vicki in a big embrace as Vicki asked, "I thought we said six thirty."

"We did. I stopped by the shop early to drop off some coursework for Lisa, and she was overrun, so I stayed to help. I can't have her collapsing before the summer's over. Good graduate students are hard to come by. I was just starting a pot of coffee."

"Well, thanks for that," said Vicki. "Another accident on 101 and Ellen was stuck in a lineup."

Kim rolled her eyes. "It's summer."

Just then Kim felt two little arms wrap around her legs. "Well, hello there," she said as she placed her hand on top of a bed of brown curls and smiled. "How's our little Hazelnut?"

"Come over, Auntie Kim, and see the new book I'm reading." Before Kim could answer, Hazel grabbed her hand and began to pull her toward the children's book section.

Kim laughed. "Okay, okay. But just for a minute because your Granny and I have some grown-up stuff to talk about."

Hazel rolled her eyes and said, "Grown-up stuff is

boring."

Vicki smiled as the two of them moved over to the corner filled with colorful books and toys while she busied herself with cleaning up the espresso counter. Her thoughts turned to how she arrived at this moment. She still considered the decision she made six years ago to buy the bookstore, right after her fifty-second birthday, a moment of madness. Her daughter agreed she'd lost her mind and pressed her not to do it.

"Sometimes your just have to leap off the cliff," Vicki told her daughter at the time.

"Oh really? This coming from Miss Patty Planner?" Eleen replied. But Vicki now heard a hint of pride when Ellen told someone her mom owned Crooked House Books.

Those first three years brought delight and disaster. For over eight years Vicki managed the shop and thought she knew all about how to run a bookstore. It didn't take long to find out she was screwed.

Cove Beach turned into a ghost town in the winter. The long winter months of rain and wind brought death to a new small business with no assets. A lesson she learned fast as her bank account drained away. Three years in and the threat of losing the shop loomed over her head. She lost count of the sleepless nights.

Not only did Vicki love Crooked House Books with all her heart, but it stood as a town landmark for over thirty-five years. To close meant not just the loss of her job, but she would fail in front of the whole town. She even heard one of her fair-weather friends call the bookstore her "midlife Maserati."

Then on a cold February day a small group of dedicated book clubbers, Kim and Meg included, walked in and saved her. They presented her with a no-strings-attached loan and all the time she needed to pay it back. *I couldn't have made it without them*, thought Vicki with a small shake of her head. Their generosity still caused a lump in her throat. This turned her thoughts to Samantha. *Something is seriously wrong. She's about to go under. I can feel it.* Vicki then squared her shoulders and picked up the coffee pot. *Not on my watch.*

"Sorry, sorry, I know I'm late." Megan Hadley said as she tromped through the back door. "There's always one last damn customer at the end of the day with a thousand questions just as you're trying to close up the greenhouses. I'm already having lurid dreams of October fifteenth when I shut the whole place down for the winter."

"Language," whispered Vicki as she tipped her head in Hazel's direction. Meg apologized, kicked off her boots by the door, and dropped down on the soft sofa just as Kim disentangled herself from Hazel's grip and took a seat in one of the wing-backed chairs. Hazel continued to babble away as she read her book to the herd of toys she set out around her feet.

"What's up?" Meg asked, as she waved her cell phone at Vicki. "I saw the bat signal, so I'm guessing it's important."

"Yes," said Vicki as she came out from the counter with three coffee cups on a tray.

"Samantha?" asked Meg.

"Yes," said Kim. "Something is clearly going on. Police cars at her place all hours of the day and night…cryptic texts that tell us nothing…now she's in Portland with Chief Porter? There has to be trouble."

"Agreed," said Vicki as she placed the tray on the coffee table in front of Meg. "But what to do about it?"

Kim and Vicki began to discuss different ways to get Samantha alone. Vicki thought a casual invitation to dinner at her house, while Kim thought it better to arrange a chance meeting in town or at the newspaper office. Meg sat with her head back against the sofa and her eyes closed until the two women finished.

"Nope. There's only one solution," Meg said as Kim and Vicki looked over at her with no small amount of apprehension at what she might say next. Meg had never been accused of being subtle. "We storm the castle."

Chapter 12

August 22 – Sunset Highway, OR

Samantha sat once again in the passenger seat of a police car as the trees lining Hwy 26 zipped by. This time a young, just-out-of-the-academy cadet, who Sam knew from around town, took the wheel. Before Mark Todd finished high school and started at the police academy, he worked every summer at Meg's garden center and bused tables at The Windswept Restaurant Friday and Saturday nights. With his practical experience almost done with the Cove Beach PD, he would soon be off to his first official post.

After she asked a few questions about school and his plans for the future, Mark babbled away. Sam let her mind drift. She missed the excitement of kids this age. The world lay at his feet, as it did for most twenty-year-olds. He could still look down the road and see all his dreams ahead of him, whereas Sam felt her dreams faded long ago. As he continued to talk about his plans to make detective, and with luck, chief one day, Sam could tell Mark knew nothing of her real identity. For Marlene and Jessica to keep her secret from the young cadet, she could have kissed them both.

In order to get Sam back to Cove Beach, Marlene and Jessica decided to have their officers meet on the road. Mark would do the bulk of the driving because it was easier to let a trainee from a small town spend the day on the road than an officer from a busy Portland station. The location for the handoff would be Scott's Drive-In in Manning, a long-standing family-run ice cream and burger place, along the Sunset Highway.

After they said their thanks and goodbyes to the Portland officer who had driven Sam out of the city, Mark paused as he opened the passenger door.

"Er," he said, with his eyes down and his forehead bright red, "would it be okay if I, um, bought a milkshake for the ride home?"

Before she could answer, he went on in a rush, "It'll only take a couple of minutes, promise."

Sam let out a genuine laugh at the question and agreed he could take his time and get whatever he wanted. When he came out of the drive-in, he had two tall cups in his hands.

"Salted caramel or blackberry?" he asked as he held up the milkshakes. She laughed again and told him she didn't care, whichever he didn't want.

"I'll give you the blackberry." He handed her the cold cup through the passenger window with a big smile. "They were just walking in with the fresh berries when I got to the counter."

He refused her offer of payment as she pulled out her wallet. "No, I've got it," he said as he blushed again but with pride in his voice. "I'm on salary now." Sam thanked him with a grin, gave his arm a squeeze, and put her wallet away.

As they pulled up to her cabin, they found another police car in the driveway.

"Good to see you again, Samantha," said Officer Tim Bennett as he put out his hand. "Did Chief Porter explain how your protection is going to work?"

Sam knew Tim from her time at the paper. He transferred from Salem to Cove Beach Police more than a decade ago.

"Yeah," said Sam as the three of them walked up to the house together. "She said an officer would be checking on me about every hour while you're on shift?"

"That's right. We won't disturb you at night, but during the day you'll probably get a knock on your door about every hour from one of us, just to make sure you're okay." Tim then said with a smile, "Not to worry. In no time at all you'll be sick of us hanging around and glad when it's over."

Sam returned the smile and showed the two men into the house. The officers checked every room and secured every door, as Tim explained to Mark what to look for while on a protection detail. Before Marlene left Portland, she explained how she didn't have the budget for around the clock protection, but she would make sure everyone would do all they could to protect her.

At the end of their search, Tim told Mark he could knock off for the day, and as the young man left, he held out a card to Sam. "I'm your night-shift officer. Use this number if you hear or see anything."

Tim left the house, and Sam breathed a sigh of relief. *Finally, I'm home.* But in the time it took her to drop her stuff on the dining room table and walk into the kitchen, she heard Aunt Dot's voice in the front garden.

"Of course, I'm going in to see Samantha. I don't care about your orders, Timothy."

Sam shook her head and grinned as she walked out to her tiny front porch. But Tim, who had known Dorothy Dixon for years, held her landlady at the front gate while he called in to the station on the radio positioned on his left shoulder. All three of them stood for a few tense moments until they heard Marlene's voice through the static. She confirmed Aunt Dot's innocence, and Tim allowed her inside.

"Well, I should say I'm innocent, for goodness' sake," said Aunt Dot, "but good on you, Timothy, for doing your duty." She reached out and patted his arm. "Can't fault you for that, but I hope there won't be any more of this nonsense each time I come over to check on Samantha?"

At her pointed look, Tim grinned. "No, never again, Mrs. Dixon. I'm way more scared of you than the chief."

Once inside the cottage and the front door closed, Dot wrapped Sam in a tight hug. The older woman held her close.

"Oh, darling, what's happened? Why are there police everywhere? And where have you been?"

Before Sam could answer, Aunt Dot pulled back and stared at her face. "Look at you! You're exhausted." The older woman then commanded, "Sit down!"

Sam tried to protest, but Dorothy cut her off. "Sit! Right now!"

Sam gave up and let herself be led to the sofa.

"I'm putting the kettle on."

Sam just sighed and leaned her head against the back of the old black and blue checkered couch and moved a matching pillow across her belly to hold tight against her body. In a few minutes she heard the tinkle of china. Sam opened her eyes. Aunt Dot then walked from the kitchen with a large tea tray in her hands. When Sam caught sight of the tray ladened with a full teapot, cups, and a sugar and creamer set, she jumped up off the couch. The older woman waved her away and continued her slow procession through the doorway.

Sam gave up and sat back down. *Oh well*, she thought, *what's the worst that could happen? A pot of tea and a creamer of milk to clean up off the old, creaky floorboards? I'm too tired to care.*

"There." Aunt Dot sat down beside Sam and put a filled teacup into her hand. "Now, tell me what in the world is going on."

Over the next hour, Sam explained what she could. Her last discussion with both Jess and Marlene sketched out a plan for who she could tell about the situation. When Sam mentioned Dorothy, Marlene stopped Jessica's protests and explained how Dorothy Dixon had been a fixture in Cove Beach for more than twenty years. And as to her ability to keep a secret, both Marlene and Sam agreed Aunt Dot would do anything to keep her renter and good friend safe once she knew the stakes. But Sam understood the need to keep quiet about the crime scene details, the letters, the similarity of the killings to old mystery novels, and her original name.

Throughout the story, Dot stared at Sam with rapt attention. Her only responses contained an "*oh!*" here and a "*my Lord!*" there. When she finished, Sam stayed quiet and let Dot take it all in. After a thirty-year career as a scientific researcher, Dorothy wouldn't race off down a path of wild speculation. Sam knew she would think before she spoke.

After a few minutes of silence, Aunt Dot said, "Well, we are just going to have to keep you safe, aren't we? Very sound of Marlene to have her bobbies keep an eye on you. Now what about you going to work? I'm not sure that's all that wise, you know."

She just listened while Aunt Dot went through all the scenarios and possible places Sam could be attacked and left for dead—both in town and along the north coast. When Dot paused to take a breath, Sam jumped in and explained she would work from home, and if she needed to go downtown, to the store or wherever, she would tell the police. That seemed to satisfy her, but Dot's furrowed brow and her clenched hands told another story. *How could she not be worried?* thought Sam. *Hell! I'm worried.*

Once alone, Sam dropped the façade of control and let the tears come. They still flowed after a long hot shower and stayed with her as she crawled into her own bed that night. She couldn't fool herself. This had only just begun. But the voice in her head, who at times served as her worse critic, stepped in and placed five words of comfort in her mind. *Right now, you are safe.* She repeated these words until she slipped off to sleep. The voice decided Samantha didn't need to hear the rest of the sentence, *if only for tonight.*

Chapter 13

August 22 – Portland, OR

At seven o'clock Colin decided to call it a day. He'd gone into the office at six thirty that morning to prepare for the staff training and then spent the rest of the day at the Cowan crime scene with Samantha and Jess.

As he made his way back to his apartment on Park Street, he thought about his nice digs. The college arranged for him to stay in a two-story townhouse close by campus, and as the name of the street implied, it faced a narrow city park that spanned several blocks. When Colin walked in for the first time, he marveled at the owner's good taste and his good luck. He could never afford something this posh back in Bournemouth.

A few days before he arrived in the States back in early August, he found out the Portland townhouse wouldn't be available right away. To bridge the gap, the college booked him into a local hotel which they assumed would solve the problem. But he asked if he could stay in one of the dorms instead.

The department chair called him the day after she read his email request. "You understand, you'll have your own studio room but share the floor with undergrads? Teenagers?"

Colin chuckled at the sound of her incredulity.

"Yes, just like the ones I'll be teaching in September." He went on when she began to protest. "It's only for three nights, and I would really like to see how your American universities work. This gives me a chance to explore the campus and find my way around." In the end she relented and booked him into a studio room on the third floor of Brookfield Hall.

Even though his time would soon end with the Portland PB, the opportunity couldn't have been better. How could he resist a chance to teach in the States and do the practical work he enjoyed so much? He hated to admit it, but two big murder cases and now maybe a third with a possible serial killer element felt like Father Christmas delivered his gifts early this year. As an academic, he spent most of his days as a talking head. Mind-numbing slides of crime scenes presented to a room full of undergrads couldn't compare to an actual investigation. Colin knew his students found some lectures just as coma-inducing as he did.

He closed his laptop, picked up the tumbler of whiskey from the coffee table, and settled back into the comfortable sofa. As he clicked through channels and the images on the screen flipped by, his mind wandered back to the last two days. He'd gone through the case file from the murder investigation five years before: the interviews, evidence, and the detectives' personal notes.

Jessica mentioned Samantha's husband dying just a few months before the first murders happened in Chinook. So, he also requested the case file of Quintin Morrill. He couldn't explain why he requested the file. But he knew a pang of compassion and respect stirred inside him for Samantha as they worked together on this case.

Even a quick scan through the file gave him a lump in his throat as he read through the sad details of her husband's death. Quintin, age fifty-two, ingested a chemical solvent used in art restoration and slipped into a coma. He never regained consciousness and died two months later. While no specific chemical signature could be found, the presence of blisters in his esophagus and rapid onset of symptoms helped the ME conclude a chemical agent. The investigation stated accidental poisoning as the cause of death. No evidence of foul play could be found. By all accounts, it seemed straightforward.

Colin couldn't help but wonder how Samantha managed to hold it all together, back then and today. He witnessed her good-natured spirit crack only twice over the past two days. His mind flashed back to the moment in the conference room when he reached out for the chair and held her arm to keep her steady when her control faltered as she made the connection in the Brignone case, and when she shouted at them all after Cowan's body had been found. All justifiable outbursts, in his opinion.

He considered Samantha to be either a very strong person or a person who failed to grasp the full reality of the situation. He hoped for the former because each successful kill makes a killer bolder and more fearless. Unless they found some evidence to connect someone to the crimes soon, he feared there would be no stopping them.

Chapter 14

August 23 – Cove Beach, OR

The next morning when Sam opened her eyes, she found her bedroom filled with sunlight. The clock on her nightstand read 8:17 a.m. She slept almost eleven hours and could still feel grittiness behind her swollen eyes and a fogginess in her brain. She swung her legs off the side of the bed and pulled on a pair of leggings and a sweatshirt. As she stood, she caught a glimpse of herself in the mirror on the wall.

"Eww," she said out loud as she reached for her favorite flat cap to hide her bedhead before she went out to the front porch.

There she found a different cop parked in the sandy driveway just on the other side of her front gate. A small female officer stepped away from her patrol car as Aunt Dot held out one of her botanical print coffee mugs. The officer took the mug just as Sam opened her front door.

"Oh, good morning, darling. So glad you were able to get some sleep last night." Dot turned and patted the officer on the arm. "I told Stephanie not to wake you. I could see your bedroom curtains were still closed. But, of course, she was so diligent, she still went all the way around the house and checked all the doors and windows at seven a.m. when she came on duty to make sure you were safe. She's just come back around to check on you again."

The blonde, thirty-something officer squeezed Dorothy's hand in return and chuckled. "That's what I'm here for, Mrs. D."

As they met at the fence, Sam opened the gate and the officer held out her hand. "I'm Officer Dean, Stephanie Dean. Not sure if you remember me? I started back in February with this station. I was in Seaview before that. I'll be the one checking in with you until seven tonight."

Sam said she did remember her and waved her into the yard. They walked down the curved stone path lined on each side with astilbes and hostas to the front porch. Their pink and purple blooms shimmied in the light breeze.

"Thank you for keeping me safe, but I'm not sure there will be much to do. The chief wants me to keep a low profile for the next couple of days. So, I'll be working from home."

"No problem. Just like Tim, I'll just be checking on you about every hour or so. Here's my cell," said Stephanie as she stepped up to give Sam her card. "Use it for any emergencies, trouble, etc. Also, if you get any calls from someone you don't know, see a person close to the house you don't recognize or shouldn't be there, or hear something, contact me or Tim right away. We don't care if it's someone walking their dog at midnight or a branch smacking against the window in the wind. Nothing's too small to be worth attention."

Once inside the house, Stephanie's eyes scanned every detail in each room. She stood only five feet tall, but even through the formless uniform and bulky bulletproof vest, Sam could see the details of her muscular arms and legs. If the killer did show up in Cove Beach, they would find a formidable opponent. As they finished the tour, Sam offered the bathroom and use of her refrigerator for drinks and food for the twelve-hour shift.

"Well, thank you, I appreciate that," Stephanie said and then flashed a sheepish grin.

"What's so funny?"

"Dorothy offered too."

A smile broadened on Sam's face. "Of course, she did, and get ready for more cups of coffee if you end up stuck with me for days on end."

Stephanie laughed. "The station is close by, but I'm thankful for the offer."

As they walked back into the living room, Sam glanced up to see Aunt Dot perched in the doorway.

Sam leaned in and whispered, "Speak of the devil. I hope you've honed your counterintelligence skills because she's a crack interrogator. She could charm the nuclear pass codes from the Pentagon's top agents."

"Everything all right, you two?" Dorothy asked with her hands gripped tight together.

"All ship-shape," said Stephanie with a big smile. As she passed by, she waved the little lady into the house and headed to her patrol car. Sam and Dot watched her back out of the narrow driveway and disappear down the back side of the dune.

Sam spoke for a few minutes with Dot and then told her that she needed to catch up on work and to check in with Mike at the paper.

"Are you sure, dear? Are you ready to be working?"

"I've got to do something to get my mind off all this insanity."

"Quite right, I suppose." She didn't look convinced but left Sam in peace.

Once alone Sam took a quick shower, fixed an easy breakfast of tea and toast, and sat down in front of her laptop. As the screen lit up, an email labeled "thank you" popped up. The romance writer gushed over Sam's last research report and told her to expect the final payment into her bank account today.

Aside from the junk mail, the other two emails looked important. The first one came from a law firm. They wanted to know if her research included criminal cases. This problem arose every once in a while. Her name came up in online searches of businesses when people dropped the word "research" in the description. Sam made a note to send back her standard "thank you, but no" form letter. Even if she did do that sort of thing, criminal case research seemed a little too close to home at the moment.

She then turned her attention to the other request. An American fiction writer, Kyle Douglas, needed help with a novel set in Great Britain around the turn of the last millennium. He hoped Sam could help him wade through the large amount of historical data he'd accumulated over the last few years when the idea for a book first sparked. Her eyes skimmed over the page until she read the last few lines of the email. She stopped, sat, and stared at the screen for several minutes. Her heart raced.

I was just talking to a friend of yours, Cornelia Cowan, at the writer's conference in Chicago this week. She gave me your name and contact info, and I wanted to get in touch.

Cornelia. Her chest ached, but Sam forced herself to read on.

She mentioned you were a freelance researcher, but she said to refer to you as "The Consulting Know-It-All"*? Said if I put that in the email, I might get your attention. I hope she's right and I didn't just completely offend you.*

A noise, a cross between a snort and a sob, jumped out of Sam's mouth. Consulting Know-It-All. CC gave her this title when Sam told her the plan to leave Chinook and change her name. She pushed the laptop aside, put her head down on her crossed arms, and wept. After the tears ran their course, she got up and grabbed a clean dish towel—the closest thing she could find—and blew her nose.

The subject line of the next email read, "Are you all right? Answer your damn cell phone!"

In a quick flash, all the things she forgot to tell Mike before the police trundled her off to the station to give a statement invaded her thoughts. *What day was that? Tuesday?* she thought as she stared at the calendar on the wall. *Was it really only two days ago? It feels like a decade.*

With all the upheaval, she forgot to pack her phone charger for the trip to Portland. She never expected to stay over, so her phone ran out of power the day before. She plugged it in on her way to bed last night but didn't turn it back on. As the screen came to life, Sam now saw three texts from Mike, one each from Kim and Meg, and two from Vicki.

A quick look at the messages from Vicki, Kim, and Meg told her those could wait. Kim's second text read,

—Why is there STILL a police car parked outside your house?— but Sam decided Mike came first. She ran through ways to apologize for the list of forgotten items while she dialed. He picked up on the second ring.

Mike skipped the niceties. "Kid! Where in the hell are you?"

"I'm back home in Cove Beach, and I'm fine."

"I've been trying to get answers out of Porter, but, kid, let me tell you, she has been holding her cards damn close to her chest. She at least let me know you were safe and under police protection. Thank God!"

It took a few more minutes to assure her grumpy bear of a boss that he didn't need to worry. She explained how her police detail worked, and that seemed to calm him down enough so they could move on to business.

"Mike, I'm so sorry, but with all the insanity I forgot to tell or pass on to you a few things that probably now need to get top priority for next week's edition. The biggest thing is the ad for the final two weekends of the play at The Gull Theater. Liz is going to be livid it didn't get into the paper this last week. I—"

Mike interrupted. "Not to worry. I caught it."

Sam let out a long sigh, and her shoulders relaxed. "Oh, I'm so glad. I know she will want a full house these next two weekends to end the summer season."

She knew with a killer out there, an ad for a small-town play shouldn't be something to stress over. But the one-hundred-seat amateur theater, with seasonal summer productions and holiday shows, stood pride of place in town. Elizabeth Weaver, the sixty-five-year-old, carotene-haired theater director, coordinated all the productions and managed the actors and volunteers. Before Liz decided to pull back and moved to Cove Beach, she spent twelve years at the impressive Oregon Shakespeare Festival in Ashland.

In the interview she gave to the paper when she first started at The Gull in January, she said she hoped to semi-retire. "I figured one more cold winter or boiling hot summer in southern Oregon would be the death of me. The mild north coast weather will be just the ticket."

Mike told Sam to make a note for one of them to interview Liz again next spring to see how well she made it through the 112 inches of annual rainfall and the 75-85 mph wind gusts of the Oregon Coast's impressive winter storms. Sam remembered Mike's words with a smile. "Let's see what she thinks about this beach paradise when the rain is smacking her sideways across the face and her roof is leaking like a sieve."

As Mike went on about Liz, something started to wiggle at the back of her mind. The theater seemed important in some way, but she couldn't say how. After a few minutes of failed concentration, she gave up. But still a memory pulled on her like a coat hem caught in a door. When you tried to move forward, it caught you up short and made you turn to look. But when she turned around, she stood alone.

Sam shook off the thought and decided to bring up the one thing they needed to talk about but shouldn't. "One more thing, Mike. Um, about me and all of this. I realize this will be the biggest news story of the year, but—"

"Let me stop you right there. Kid, you are up to

your ass in alligators, and we all know that. I'm not going to run anything until it's confirmed you're safe. Besides, I'm expecting an exclusive—that's for damn sure." Mike ended with a hoot of laughter.

Sam smiled and imagined the big grin on her boss' face. "You'll have to talk to my agent." Mike snorted and hung up.

Before the call, she decided not to mention the Alvarez murder in Chicago. Not only because of the promise she made to Jessica, but because she knew Mike would still have contacts at one or more of the city newspapers where he used to work and with the Chicago PD. A part of her itched for more information, but another part knew she and Mike would be in a shitload of trouble if the Portland police found out. But, on the flipside, her boss would blow a gasket when he came to realize the Chicago murder connection if she didn't tell him.

Sam sat and stared out the window for almost ten minutes before she picked up her phone and called Mike back. She took it on faith that if Mike said he wouldn't print anything until this nightmare ended, he meant it.

"Hey, kid, whatcha forget?"

Sam paused for one final moment. *Tell him you butt dialed*, said the voice in her head, *and hang up*.

"Mike, you have still contacts in Chicago?"

Over the next twenty minutes, Sam and Mike discussed Alicia's death. Sam tiptoed around the more sensitive details but gave the old bloodhound enough to get started.

"So, what you're telling me is this Alicia Alvarez was murdered in the hospital in June? The two of you used to work together at Duniway. You are thinking there's a link?"

Sam drew out each letter of her response. "P-o-s-s-i-b-l-y…"

"Yup. Say no more. I'll make a few calls and see what I can find."

"And Mike—"

"Got it, kid. This is between you, me, and the cottonwood tree."

After the call ended, she checked her phone and found two missed calls from Marlene at the same time she heard a knock on her door. Stephanie stood on her porch. Sam dialed Marlene and walked to the door with the phone in her hand. She put the phone on speaker and explained why she didn't answer when the chief called, and to call off search and rescue.

But before she hung up the phone and Stephanie left the house, she decided to tell them about the email. The writer's name, Kyle Douglas, meant nothing to her, and she didn't see a connection, but the letter did mention him meeting with CC in Chicago.

Stephanie walked straight to the laptop and asked Sam to please open the email from Douglas. The three of them discussed the contents after Sam forwarded it to Marlene at the police station.

"I'll make sure Noguchi has the information," Marlene said, "so she can assign someone to track down the writer and confirm his story, attendance, and alibi. Please don't respond to him until all has been clarified. Okay?" Sam agreed.

"Now, brace yourself."

Sam closed her eyes and held her breath.

"Another letter arrived this morning in your PO box."

Chapter 15

August 23 – Cove Beach, OR

As Stephanie pulled her patrol car into the city hall parking lot, Sam noticed a group of locals on the sidewalk. They watched as she got out of the front passenger seat. She avoided eye contact and tried to look casual while she thanked the gods Stephanie let her ride in the front seat. To be seen in the back of a police car would make for great gossip. She didn't even want to think of the rumors that were already flying around town.

The two of them moved to the far side of the parking lot and through the small door marked Cove Beach Police Station. Then, all of a sudden, a thought hit her right in the face. *What happens if this story breaks and it's not The Chronicle who breaks it?* She spent all morning focused on Mike, not the whole world of news and reporters. Sam stopped in the middle of the hallway. *It could all start again, like before.*

"Everything all right?" asked Stephanie.

"What? Oh, yeah, sorry." Sam looked up and forced a small smile.

Sam stepped forward, and the two continued into the station. She forced that worry to the back of her brain and told herself, *Just deal with one fucked-up moment at a time.*

Marlene glanced up from the evidence bag on her desk as the two women appeared in the squad room. Marlene opened her door and with a wave ushered them both into her office. Sam sat down in one of the chairs Marlene pointed to across from her desk.

"Thanks, Steph. Go ahead and get back on patrol. I'll radio when you can pick Sam back up and take her home." Stephanie left, and Marlene shut the door.

She then leaned over and picked up the clear plastic evidence bag from her desk. Marlene hesitated for just a moment and then handed it to Sam. She reached out and then hesitated.

"Go ahead. It's been printed, photographed, and cataloged. Noguchi has a digital image. You have every right to see it. Just don't take it out of the bag."

Sam could see through the clear plastic to the opened envelope. Like a red stop light, the wax seal glowed. As she turned the whole packet over, familiar yellowed parchment paper, scrolled font, and signature at the bottom stared back at her. She took a deep breath and forced her eyes down to the words on the page.

Hello Samantha,

What do you think of my handywork? How many have you figured out? Only one? Your good, good friend CC? What a tragedy. So vital, so full of life. No longer young, of course, but it's always a shock. Isn't that what they say? So shocking! Not to me. Her fate was sealed when she picked you. What is so special about you?

The others (oh yes, there are others) are playing the supporting cast in this story. Have you made the connection yet? I'm thinking, no. If you had, the police would be knocking at my door.

I wonder what will happen in Act Three.

Fiction is so much easier to "detect" than real life, isn't it?

Deadly Yours

"You okay?" asked Marlene.

"Yeah," Sam croaked. Her mouth seemed to be filled with cotton. She sat up straighter in the chair and cleared her throat. "Yes, fine."

Marlene looked doubtful as she handed Sam a bottle of water from her office fridge. "Noguchi is having Davies analyze it alongside the other letters. The first one from Tuesday and the two others from five years ago. One or two letters—data points—of the killer's voice doesn't give a profiler much to go on, but this current letter could really help jump this case forward."

Sam just nodded, as she kept her eyes on the note. "You know there are a lot of references to a performance or play in this one, aren't there?"

"Does that mean anything to you?"

"I'm not sure. Something has been pestering me all morning. I can't put my finger on what it is. It's driving me insane." Sam growled, "*Arrgh! What is it?*"

"Don't force it. You've had one heck of a week. Trust that it will come to you."

Sam started to share her thoughts on this being some piece of drama when Marlene's desk phone began to ring. "This will be Noguchi. She was going to read the letter and then get in touch with both of us."

Marlene pushed the button for line two and said, "Morning, Detective. Go ahead. I have Sam here, and you are on speaker."

"Morning, Chief. Great, thanks. Sam, how are you

doing?"

"Fine. All's quiet here."

"That's good to hear. So, this is what's happening on this end. Colin is combing through the letters and going back over the crime scene data to see what he can make of the killer. Now, Marlene, I'm not going to speculate as to a serial aspect. I don't want to bring in the FBI if I don't have to. Since I have a criminal profiler right here in the office, I'm going to use his skills before we leap to any conclusions.

"And," Jessica said, just as Samantha opened her mouth to explain again how the three killings must be connected, "before you jump in here, Sam, I know that you think they are all related. I get it, and you may just be right. But we need to go through all the evidence and procedures to see if there is a link. Chief Porter will tell you, evidence first. Assumption and bias are the quickest way to fail in a case like this, got it?"

Marlene nodded her head at Sam and said, "Right. Detective, Sam might have something new to go on. Let's us three discuss it here before we move forward. Sam, explain what you picked up from this last letter—"

Jessica cut in. "Hold that thought for a minute. I'll want Davies in on this. Be right back."

In less than a minute, Colin's voice came through the speaker. "Jessica says you have thoughts on this newest letter?"

Sam went on to explain how there seemed to be a lot of theater references in this second letter. "So, I see phrases like 'a tragedy,' 'supporting cast,' 'act three,' that sort of thing. No idea if it's important, but that's what hit me in this one."

Sam made it clear that in all the time she taught at Duniway, she never covered plays. She told them she would sometimes touch on Agatha Christie's mysteries originally written as a play or adapted into plays later, but the class didn't focus on the performance aspect, only the stories themselves.

Marlene asked, "What made you think about the theater? Was it just the letter? Because I look at this and my mind goes to the movies or TV." She then chuckled. "Maybe that makes me lowbrow, but I don't instantly think of a play."

"Well, to be honest it's something that's been tapping on me since this morning after I talked with Mike about Liz and The Gull's ad for the last two weekend performances."

Sam and Marlene stopped to explain Mike, Elizabeth Weaver, and The Gull Theater to the two on the other end of the phone. Sam said, "I suppose, it could just be because that was the last thing I was thinking about before I came into the station and read the letter."

"Hmm, maybe," said Colin, "but I'm thinking it might be worth looking into. Could all be rubbish, but there are no bad ideas at this point."

"Chief," said Jessica, "how much do you know about Weaver?"

The conversation went on to outline the director's background. Sam filled in the blanks from what she could remember from the interview.

"Wait a minute," said Jessica, "are you saying Weaver has been in town less than a year?"

"Yes," said Marlene and Sam at the same time.

"Less time than you have, but you didn't know

her?"

"No," said Sam, "sorry, yes—less time than me—no, I didn't know her."

"Huh, I still think it sounds a little too convenient. Chief, could someone on your end talk to Weaver? Colin and I are in interviews all day with Sam's old college colleagues, a couple of past students, and you're in Cove Beach on the spot."

"Not a problem."

"One more thing," said Sam as she reread the letter again. "I just noticed a difference between the letters before and the ones now. Sorry I didn't catch it earlier."

Colin jumped in. "What is it, Samantha?"

"Last time, and Jess correct me if I'm wrong, last time the first letter arrived before the bodies were found. But these new letters are being sent after a murder. Right?"

Everyone sat silent for a moment.

"Jess?" asked Sam.

"Yes, you're right. Let me just take a look at the old file notes to be sure."

"So, if that's right, then the killer isn't taking any chances at being found out before a murder is committed," said Colin. "This could signify a change in behavior which isn't unusual for a serial killer as they learn from past experiences."

"It seems to me," said Sam, "that he's just getting smarter. I wouldn't announce a murder for fear I'd get caught before I could commit it. Or, like last time the one you want to antagonize—me—gets the hell out of town and you're left with no one to stalk."

"Well, I won't bore anyone with the psychology behind why a killer would want to announce his intentions," Colin said. "But I will say that it's mostly to do with a heightened sense of excitement and the need to ramp up the fear in the person they're tormenting."

After a few more minutes of discussion, Colin agreed to go back over the file notes and see if this change could help with leads.

"Now, AJ—oops, sorry, did it again—Samantha. Colin and I have been talking, and we think it might be a good idea if you see the interviews we're conducting with people from your Duniway days," Jessica said.

Sam moved to the edge of her seat. She opened her mouth to tell Jessica she could be back in Portland in a couple of hours. Jessica's next words stopped her before she could speak. "But don't get too excited. You aren't going to get anywhere near them."

She then went on to explain their plan for Sam to watch the interviews through the police department's secure video conferencing program.

"Thanks to Covid, it's now a virtual world," said Marlene, "and believe it or not, even here in little Cove Beach we are not without technology. We can video conference with the best of them."

Through the speaker, Sam heard both Jessica and Colin laugh.

Jess said, "No mail delivery, but there's Wi-Fi. Go figure."

"Shocking, I know," added Marlene with a smile.

"Chief, I've also sent you the ME report on Cowan."

"Yup, I saw it this morning."

"Sam, I'm going to let the chief run through it with you. If you see any similarities to these mysteries, or anything like that let me…no, wait…let me think…let Colin know. He's going to be more able to take calls and texts today than I will."

"Of course."

Colin piped up. "Text me first, please, Samantha. It will be less of a disruption. Then I'll step away and call or text you back."

After a few more details about the interview process, the call ended. Both Marlene and Sam sat in silence for a few moments, then the chief got up and walked around to her desk and pulled up the report. She turned her screen toward Sam, and they studied the medical examiner's summary together.

The report stated a clear cause of death. Cornelia died from strychnine which caused her body to convulse and go into rigor much quicker than if she had been killed without the drug.

"What's MDMA?" asked Sam as she flipped through the toxicology section of the report. "It says here that CC's stomach and bloodstream also contained MDMA. Oh, and small traces were found in the sink along with coffee and strychnine. I knew something was dumped down the sink."

"MDMA is ecstasy, the date rape drug. Sometimes called 'molly.' "

"Jesus! Why?"

Not that Sam didn't know about ecstasy, anyone on any campus around the world knew about the date rape drug. But how it fit in with CC's death, she couldn't understand.

Marlene stared into Sam's confused eyes and paused before she answered the question. She went on in a low, calm voice. "It can be used to subdue someone…make them compliant. That would have given the strychnine time to go into effect."

Sam's face hardened. "*Compliant?* What a fucker this guy is!"

Marlene nodded but decided not to tell Sam how much pain her friend would have been in from the strychnine right before she died. No one needed to hear that, ever. That's why cops and coroners used phrases like, "death would have been instantaneous," "they died in their sleep," and "with that level of drugs in their system, they wouldn't have felt a thing." These little white lies made it easier on friends and relatives who loved this once living and breathing person.

Marlene scanned down Julie Carl's report and read out the key points.

"Also found in the system…small amounts of a derivative of *Atropa belladonna* root, commonly known as deadly nightshade…quantity not sufficient to be main cause of death. Final Conclusion: victim first incapacitated with 3,4-Methylenedioxy-methamphet-amine."

Marlene paused, looked over at Sam and smiled. "Say that fast five times. That's the long name for MDMA. Cause of death: strychnine poisoning. Make anything out of that?"

"Yes." A long sigh came from Samantha. She knew it the minute Marlene said *Atropa belladonna*. She reached for her cell and called Colin. When he answered, she put him on speaker and explained the importance of the ancient botanical mentioned in the report.

"The presence of belladonna root is believed to be the closest plant anyone can equate to the fictitious devil's foot used in the Sherlock Holmes story. Not in the shape, but the effects. Now in the story the dried root was burned, and the victims inhaled the fumes. Some died, some just went nuts."

"Bugger me," said Colin after a moment of silence.

"Yes. This probably confirms what you and I suspected at the crime scene. This was a reenactment of *The Adventures of the Devil's Foot*. The 1910 story, published in a long-gone British magazine called *The Strand*. The strychnine caused the death and unusual rigor, but the belladonna and the candle were clearly added by the killer, for no other reason than as a deliberate clue."

"Why wouldn't the killer have just used the belladonna? Why the strychnine also?" asked Colin.

"I'm no expert, but from what little I do know, it's because it doesn't work fast enough or guarantee death. That's why there's never been a definitive on it as the drug Conan Doyle refers to in the story."

"Remind me of the motivation of that crime in the book."

"Simple greed and malice."

The call ended.

Marlene sent Sam off with Stephanie, and she made her way to The Gull to find Liz Weaver at the theater. The troupe would be gathering in a few hours for the Friday performance, so she hoped to catch the director in her office.

Back in the patrol car, Stephanie and Sam inched their way through the downtown traffic.

"When we get back, is it okay if I sneak down to the beach? Two minutes, promise."

"Going stir crazy already?" Stephanie laughed. "It

hasn't even been twenty-four hours. It normally takes people a lot longer to get tired of me."

Sam grinned. "It's not you. I just need to see the ocean."

"I get it, but I can't really have you on an open beach with only me to take the bullet." When she saw the look of shock and concern on Sam's face, Stephanie laughed again and raised a hand. "Not that I'm thinking there's a sniper hiding in the dunes. No. But it isn't the safest place for me to protect you."

As they pulled up to the weatherworn picket fence, Stephanie went in to check the cabin. Sam agreed to wait on the porch. With an "all clear" Sam stepped forward over the threshold.

"Sam, Stephanie," said a familiar voice from around the side of the big house. "You two come over for a spot of lunch on the deck."

"Did you catch that? It wasn't a question. There's no turning her down," said Sam as she smiled and waved to the silver-haired commander.

The two women didn't argue. They walked together to the big house. Sam leaned over and whispered, "Well, at least I'll get my beach fix."

As they rounded the corner of the beachfront house, Stephanie understood what Sam meant. The two stood on the top of the high dune and stared. The sun shone bright on the shore, and the entire Pacific Ocean lay at their feet. Sam's eye scanned the horizon. A bank of dark purple clouds stretched both north and south. A storm was coming.

Chapter 16

August 23 - Portland, OR

Colin returned to the conference room after Samantha and the chief confirmed their suspicions of Cowan's death and the use of belladonna. Jessica walked in with the details of the Alvarez murder she received from the Chicago PD. Officer Calhoun stood at the large whiteboard and added these new notes to the wall as Jessica called them out. The three murder cases now hung side by side on the wall.

Colin enjoyed the back and forth between colleagues as they went over the possible scenarios. He knew profiles worked only if evidence and discussion occurred amongst a group of diverse investigators. One person's view would always slant one way or another due to their background, experience, and personal bias. He'd seen it time and time again. The lead detective gets a theory stuck in their head, and then evidence is either disregarded or given far too much weight.

As a woman of color, Jessica's Japanese and African American parents gave her a certain insight. Whereas Colin's British ancestry and upbringing gave him the outsider's perspective. Their opposite backgrounds and experiences only strengthened the investigation. Colin considered Jacob Calhoun the voice somewhere in the middle. At just twenty-four,

Jacob's strides to make a place for himself amongst the detective team could be tied to Jess's guidance and leadership. A serial case would define the type of cop he could be going forward. That's if it didn't all turn into one big cock-up.

"So, what have we got?" said Jess as she waved a hand at the wall in front of her now crammed with photos, reports, and notes. Jacob stayed silent, so Colin began.

"All right, we know the killer is meticulous. Even if we set aside Samantha's theory that these are all related killings mimicking old murder mysteries, there's no way around the level of planning that went into all of them. You don't just show up at a hospital and wrap surgical tubing around someone's neck on a whim. So, I believe the killer is probably well educated and of above average intelligence."

"Still thinking a man?" asked Jess as she glanced down at her phone.

"Hmm, not sure just yet. These letters are keeping me guessing. They seem to be more female than male. But if the killer is as smart as we think, then that could be the point of how they are written. Serials can be a bugger to nail down when they don't completely fit a tried and tested profile."

"Calhoun? What's your take?" Jess put her phone away and turned toward the younger officer. He stood at the whiteboard with his arms crossed. He didn't speak for a moment.

"I just don't know. With the evidence showing two victims drugged before death by the killer, or not in the case of Alvarez with pre-op drugs, that could be a man or a woman. Brignone…no drugs. But to be honest, and no criticism of your profiling work, Mr. Davies, I think we are getting ahead of ourselves. What we need to establish right now are means and opportunity and push the why to the back burner."

"Agreed," said Jessica, "so let's go figure out who had the means and opportunity. Text just came through. We have Paul Neilson in interrogation room B."

Jess conferred with the tech team about streaming the interviews for Chief Porter, and then everyone took their positions. Colin stood behind the two-way mirror while Jessica and Jacob went into the next room to begin the questioning. Paul Neilson now stared back at Colin through the mirror.

Jessica welcomed and thanked the forty-nine-year-old man with strawberry-blond hair for coming into the station. She apologized for the forty-minute drive into Portland for the discussion as she took a seat across from the suspect. Jacob entered the room and offered Neilson a bottle of water as he placed it on top of the square table. Then he sat down in the chair to the man's left.

Colin smiled as he watched the two detectives place themselves around the table as if ready to have a casual chat. The small space on the other side of the mirror didn't look like an interrogation room at first glance. It contained an old chalkboard mounted to the wall and a small mirror positioned over a waist-high bookcase along the other. The "person of interest" would notice the small cameras in the ceiling in each of the four corners, but these days people expected to see cameras everywhere, especially in a police station.

"Paul, we just need to talk with you about a statement you gave," said Jess as she paused to look at her notes, "hmm, let's see, five years ago about the murders on campus of the three graduate students."

Colin listened but didn't hear anything new in the man's statement. He shifted his attention instead to the man himself. As he watched this soft-spoken, somewhat effeminate person, he noticed Paul showed only mild surprise at Jessica's request. Colin paid close attention to Paul's long, pale fingers as they reached out and opened the water bottle. He took a very small sip, replaced the cap, and then dabbed his lips with a handkerchief he pulled from his pocket. Colin's brow creased as he jotted down, *Who carries handkerchiefs anymore?* The profiler also took note of his pressed shirt and pants and the beige blazer Paul placed over the back of his chair with extreme care when he first sat down. Colin added *Fastidious* to his notes.

As Jess concluded the questions about the old case, Paul asked, "I'm sorry, but why is this all coming up again? Do you have new leads? Have you found out who did that horrible thing at Duniway?"

Jess didn't answer as she folded over a new sheet on her legal pad which revealed a long list of additional questions. After three years working with Jessica, Jacob understood his cue to step in.

"Possibly, so that's why we are reinterviewing anyone who was close to the people back then."

"But I wasn't close to the students. I didn't even know those kids."

"We understand that," Jacob continued, "but you did know an Anna Jean Morrill."

Paul suddenly became more alert. "AJ? Is she all right? I heard about Cornelia's death on the news. Is she…? Has she been…?"

"So, you knew Cornelia Cowan?" asked Jacob.

"More by reputation. I only saw her a few times. Everyone knew of Cornelia. She published many of the Duniway textbooks and PhD dissertations. Along with the popular press side of things. The Upton Press offices are located about a half mile away from the main campus, so we didn't come into contact with each other very often."

Both Jess and Jacob paused for a moment to see if Neilson would volunteer any additional information on the murder victim. When he stayed silent, Jessica tried a different tack. "When was the last time you spoke to Ms. Morrill?"

Paul, who had leaned forward toward the two detectives when first asked about AJ, now sat back in his chair. He looked bewildered by the sudden change back to Anna Jean. "I…when was it? W-e-e-l-l." The college administrator drew out the word making it almost sound like "wheel." "If we are looking at five years ago when the students were killed, then four years since I've seen or talked to her? I think that's right."

The distinctive sound of his voice roused Colin from his notes. He jotted down a reminder to ask one of the detectives if this was a type of American dialect or accent. If so, he'd never heard it spoken before.

"Can you tell us about that last time?" asked Calhoun.

"Well, it must have been on campus the day she packed up her office."

"Would this be the office she shared with other colleagues at Duniway?" asked Jessica.

"No, she had her own office by then. We put her in the history department, I think, because spots were so hard to find."

Paul then went on to explain without being asked, "Once you get your PhD and are considered a full faculty member, then we try to do what we can to give you your own office space. It gives the full professors a bit more status and privacy for meeting with students during office hours, doing research, that sort of thing. The history department is in the same building as English Lit, so there's a lot of mixing and mingling throughout."

"Understood. About that last day…?" Jess asked.

"Oh yes, yes. Well, I was stopping by to get her keys, to tell her the college president wanted to see her before she left, and to let her know how much everyone would miss her."

"Is that true?" Jacob asked.

Paul paused for a minute as his brows came together and his eyes narrowed. Then his face went scarlet, and he raised his voice. "What do you mean? That's what happened, what I did!"

Jess's eyes swung up from her notes to assess Paul's sudden reaction.

"No," chuckled Jacob as he put up his hands in mock surrender to help give the man a false sense of ease. "Sorry, I wasn't questioning what you remembered. I was asking, was it true Ms. Morrill would be missed at Duniway?"

Pau relaxed and said, "Oh, I see. Well, yes. AJ was liked by most everyone, students and staff. She was a real asset to the Lit department too. Her classes on mystery literature and true crime were a big draw. When you pack 'The Pit,' "—he chuckled under his breath—"the administration pays attention."

When the two officers just stared at his last comment, Paul said, "Oh, sorry. 'The Pit' is the big, 220 seat theater in Anthony Hall. It's so deep and the stairs so steep, I get vertigo in there."

"You said 'liked by most everyone'?" asked Jess as she put the emphasis on "most."

"Well, you are always going to have a few students who get a bad grade and complain about professors. Especially if they come from money." He motioned quotation marks in the air when he said "money." "Those kids are always the worst, and it's become chronic these days. Most administration time is spent placating parents about their underachieving little cherubs."

"Ah," said Jacob, "anyone at the college who didn't find AJ so easy to like?"

Paul shook his head. He went on to say he couldn't remember any trouble until those horrible letters started arriving.

"It was all too much. AJ just couldn't take it any longer. And how could you blame her? It happened just a year or so after her husband's death." He shook his head again and looked down at his hands. "Such a tragedy."

"Tragedy?" asked Jess. She let the word ooze out to see if Paul would react. She remembered that word being used in the last letter. She remained silent but didn't take her eyes off his face.

The older man started off again with what Jess thought must be his favorite word. "W-e-e-l-l, wasn't it? To have just gotten back to a full schedule of classes? After taking time off the year before to be there for her dying husband, and begin her next research project only to be knocked down once again with those students being murdered and some maniac telling her it was her fault?" Both Jess and Jacob now descended on the timid man. They pelted him with questions as to how he would know AJ was to blame and what exactly he knew about the killer.

"I read the first letter, for goodness' sake!" Paul shouted. Both detectives remained stoic, but inside they celebrated. They rattled him.

His voice rose, and his breathing became more labored. He went on to explain how the first letter appeared in the college mail and had been routed to the English Lit department. "I was there in her office when she opened it. I was even the one to put the letter in her interoffice mailbox, along with everyone else's mail that day. And, like I said in my original meeting with the police, it looked like a wedding or graduation invitation. The bodies of those poor theater students were found the very next morning."

Jessica's head snapped up. "Theater students?"

She grabbed a stack of notes from the file in front of her and flipped through them as her eyes darted back and forth over the pages. *What did Samantha say about a theatrical feel to the letter?*

"I don't remember any mention of the victims' majors," Jess said. They both sat silent and waited for the reply.

Paul stared first at Jessica and then at Jacob and wondered, *Are these two messing with me?* He thought he recognized the female detective from the investigation before, but he couldn't be sure after all these years. *Did they not even read their own notes?*

"It was printed in the student newspaper, *The Daily*

Duniway, at the time. You didn't know? The murders were covered for days on campus."

Jess sat there for a moment as her mind went back to that first fucked-up investigation. Her boss, Herb Shively, had been such a dick throughout the whole thing. It didn't surprise her that something like this got missed. He relegated her to busywork because Shively didn't want her quote, "getting in the way of *his* investigation," unquote. Jess knew being assigned to one of the last good ol' boys on the force had been a test.

As he counted down the days to retirement, Herb would disappear for two-hour lunches and be out the door as the clock struck five, not a minute later. She told herself that if she could just refrain from kneeing him in the balls every time he opened his mouth to make some snide remark about her sex or race, she could have a career. *Amazing what a few years, and the #MeToo movement, could do to straighten out a backward system*, she thought.

After a few more questions about the students, they moved on to find out Paul's whereabouts during the other three murders, and then Jess concluded the interview. If his alibi checked out, then he couldn't have been in Chicago in June. But this didn't completely rule him out as a suspect in Jessica's mind. Her experience told her the Chicago murder might be a hired job. She made a note to discuss that with her team later.

As Jacob escorted Paul out of the station, he put a hand on his shoulder and thanked him once again for all his cooperation. When he returned to the conference room a few minutes later, Jess said, with a wide smile,

"Nice touch with that 'Mr. Thank You So Much' there at the end. He was probably thinking you were his new best friend by the time he got to his car."

Jacob laughed and said, "Isn't that what you always say, 'make them feel at ease,' 'make them happy'? I even got a 'W-e-e-l-l, nice to meet you' at the end." Jess gave a snort.

As Colin stepped into the room, he said, "Well, this is a sight." At that the two laughed harder. "What?"

Jess waved a hand at the two men as she grinned. "Okay, okay, what's next?"

"Priscilla Greene," said Jacob, "she's in the building."

Chapter 17

August 23 - Cove Beach, OR

"A spot of lunch" with Aunt Dot ended up as a full spread of iced tea, sandwiches, and cake all served on her picnic table under a large blue awning that matched her house shutters. They both protested all the food and effort, but Dorothy brushed them away with a wave. "It was no bother. Now sit down and tuck in."

"I'm really sorry, Mrs. Dixon, but I'm on duty."

"Stephanie, dear, do you really think someone is going to come charging around the corner in broad daylight?" Aunt Dot then poured iced tea into three tall, frosty glasses.

Stephanie chuckled but didn't take her eyes off the narrow driveway between the homes. "Ah, but what if they do and I'm sitting here eating cake? Not a good way to impress Chief Porter, that I do know."

Dot fussed until Stephanie accepted a sandwich to take back to her car. Stephanie told Samantha she'd do a quick search of her cabin and then get back on patrol. With a wave and a "thank you" she disappeared.

About thirty minutes later, Sam told Dot she needed to get to work. The two of them carried the lunch tray into the house, and after Aunt Dot refused her offer to help with the dishes, Sam returned home.

Sam sat at her laptop but couldn't keep a single

thought in her head. She didn't want to sit and think about these three people from her past life dead. But that's all her brain would focus on—death and the newest letter.

While she waited for the streaming trouble with the interviews to be fixed, Jess asked Samantha to take the time to think back to anything or anyone she'd angered or upset by her success. Jessica believed the person writing the letters held a grudge over the former professor's advancement at Duniway. Colin agreed but wanted her to consider the mention of Sam being picked by Cornelia in the second letter.

As she looked back at her time at Duniway College, she couldn't remember anyone ever being openly hostile about her classes or her research. But when egos and type A personalities with advanced degrees all end up under one roof in a university environment, then snideness and pissing matches are common. Nothing specific came to mind.

Maybe, she thought, *there's a different way to approach this*. She texted Colin once again, and he called her back in less than a minute.

As she heard Colin's British accent through the phone, an involuntary flutter moved up her spine. It left her confused as she shook it off and concentrated on the call.

"Hello, Samantha. You are probably wondering how the interviews are going? A bit of a technical nightmare on this end, so you probably won't be sitting in until tomorrow. Sorry."

"When it comes to IT, I've stopped asking why. But I'm calling to see if I can run an idea past you."

"Of course. How can I help?"

"I'm guessing someone is going through CC's office?"

"Yes, Jessica sent down one of her officers from here to work with the local Chinook police yesterday. They should be almost done."

"Could the crime scene officers check and see if they can find CC's 'reject' file? I know she kept certain ones because she never knew when they might submit another manuscript. She liked to go back and compare their old work with the new submission."

By her own design, Cornelia appeared as a tyrant and a hard-ass. But deep down she hoped the writers would take her edits to heart and become better over time and get published. She held a soft spot for unpublished writers—her dirty little secret.

Sam remembered a day in CC's office. She said, "I want them all to get a book deal. Just so they can have the big pat on the back they all crave." Then she would sigh and toss the manuscript onto the rejection stack. "But, Jesus, some of these people really shouldn't be allowed a laptop!"

"Maybe there's someone CC decided not to publish?" said Sam to Colin. "Or, gave some bad feedback to? I know it's a long shot, but..." Her voice trailed off. She tried not to sound desperate.

"No, I'd say that's rather a good idea. Was this done before in connection with the letters and threats five years ago?"

"I don't know. But I do know CC kept her own submission notes in that file too. I've seen it in her office. Let's just say the former lead detective, Jess's boss back then, was...umm... well..."

"An arsehole?"

Sam couldn't stop a burst of laughter. "Yes, and then some. How did you know?"

"I've been reading through the old case notes, and in the paper file there are some handwritten notes by Shively. A real gormless prat. No listening to anyone."

Sam didn't know the definition of a gormless prat, but it sounded right.

"That's how I felt every time we met. He didn't respect me or any woman that I could see. And it was his idea or nothing. I finally gave up and just worked with Jessica in the end. She's even the one who told me to get the hell out of Chinook when the investigation stalled about six months after the students were killed and a second letter arrived."

After her call with Colin, where he ended their discussion only after Sam agreed to get some rest, she saw a missed call from Mike. He picked up on the first ring.

"So, just how far in the crapper are you?"

"Why? What did you find out?"

"Not a lot but what I did find out circled me back to Brignone's death."

Shit, Sam thought as she put her hand to her temple. *I told you so,* said the voice in her head. *Should have gone with the butt-dial excuse.*

"Okay, shoot."

Mike went on to explain how his metro contact led him to his old cop contact and how that led to a security guy his contact knew at the hospital. The spiderweb spiraled out from there. As he started to talk, Sam grabbed a legal pad from the table. Her hand flew across the page. She gave up all hope of correct spelling, punctuation, and sentence structure just to keep up.

"I don't even know where to start," said Sam as she stared down at the six pages of scribbles in front of her.

"Kid, let me tell you, neither do I, but what I do know is that a person was seen walking away from Alvarez's body right before her death was discovered."

"A person? Well, that's great. If there's an ID then—"

"I'll stop you right there. No go on the ID. All they saw was a person in scrubs leaving through a door leading to the service stairwell. But get this, the security guard saw someone coming out of the stairwell into the parking garage at about the right time dressed all in black. Of course, the person wore a hoodie, dark glasses, the whole bit, so no telling if it was a man, woman, black, white, young, or old. All they got was that the person stood about five-seven and trim. But at least it's something."

"Yeah, it's something."

They both sat silent for a moment.

"But wait," said Sam, "how did that bring you back to Bob Brignone?"

"It's the Duniway connection. Chicago PD is looking into Alvarez's past for any leads, just like they're probably doing with you. My contact is telling me that they have struck out on linking up anyone in her Chicago circle of friends and family. As they widened the search, Brignone's murder popped up and seems too convenient. I also know they've been in touch with Portland police about the case."

"Mike, I should probably stop you right there. If you keep digging, you and I will be in for a world of hurt from the police detective on the case here in

Oregon."

"What am I always telling you? We don't work for them. So, here's the bad news. The press in Chicago are sniffing around."

"*Shit!*"

"Before you set your hair on fire, I've asked for a little cooperation from my friends at the paper. They'll sit on it until there's a story to tell. A college dean's death is newsworthy but not a high priority in a city like Chicago. So, you and I should be safe for the moment."

"Oh, Mike, you're the best. What a relief."

"Wait. There's a catch."

"Hit me."

"You are going to have to give my contact an interview when the dust settles. After the one you're giving me, of course. But if you get one call before that from any reporter, say nothing, hang up, and let me know. I'll handle them."

Chapter 18

August 23 – Cove Beach, OR

Sam's stomach growled as she hung up with Mike. *What in the world do I have in the house for dinner?* she thought as she got up from the table and made her way into the kitchen. Just as she opened the refrigerator door, she stopped. She heard voices on her porch. An uneasiness moved across her back.

She left the blue and black checked curtain pulled back this morning and could now see the back of Stephanie's head. She couldn't see who else might be on the porch because on either side of her front door, rectangular stained-glass windows blocked her view. The windows stood shoulder level and showed an inlaid scene of the sun setting over the ocean with shades of blues and greens at the bottom and moved to brilliant yellows and oranges toward the top of each frame. Aunt Dot put them in for privacy, so no one from the driveway could look straight into the renter's living room.

Sam stepped up to the clear window in the door to get a better look. She could now see around Stephanie's shoulders to a group of women stopped at her front gate. With a long exhale, she relaxed her shoulders and smiled. The book clubbers. As Sam went to open her front door, Stephanie's hand tightened on the doorknob.

"Samantha, I need you to stay inside your home until I have cleared these people with Chief Porter."

The seriousness of Stephanie's voice made Sam take a step back from the door. To break the tension, Sam said, "Sure. I get it. They look highly suspicious to me."

At that the visitors laughed, but they all stayed by the front gate. No one wanted to do anything that might escalate the situation. Stephanie didn't move her left hand from the doorknob, nor her right hand, which Sam couldn't see, from her holster.

Sam's worry went straight to Kim. She knew she could take care of herself, but the sudden knot in Sam's stomach still pulled tight. She peeked out the window just in time to watch Meg and Vicki each take a slight step forward and put their bodies between Stephanie and Kim. Even though Kim stared right over the top of their heads, a warm relief spread through her body, and a lump formed in her throat. *I love these women.*

After a few more tense moments, Marlene's voice came over the radio and Stephanie's erect posture changed. "Okay," said Stephanie with a smile and a nod, as she took her hand off the pistol and moved away from the door. "You can go in. Just had to be sure. Thank you for your cooperation."

"Of course," said Vicki as she walked up the path to the door with her arms wrapped around a pink cake box from the Beach House Bakery and two bottles of Shiraz.

"Not a problem at all," said Kim behind her. "She should have been put under house arrest years ago." She carried a pizza box with a roll of paper towels and a stack of paper plates balanced on top.

At that came a snort from Meg, who walked through the door with a potted plant in one hand, a tub of vanilla bean ice cream in the other, and a jar of hot fudge tucked in her armpit. "We've known it all along. She's been shifty from the start. Never trusted her."

Once in the house, Sam found herself in a bear hug with Meg, followed by Kim and Vicki. Then she watched as the invasion began with a flurry of activity. The three women bustled this way and that to get all the food and drinks settled. Sam guessed it would be a long siege.

"Wow!" said Sam as she noticed Kim's short hair for the first time. "You did it. You shaved off your braids. Let's see the back."

Kim turned around to expose her long, bronze neck. Her skin glowed against the upturned collar of her white shirt.

"Now that's sexy."

Kim put her hand up to the back of her neck and touched the close-clipped curls at the nape. Her hair shone black with touches of gray.

"You know, I almost didn't do it." She laughed. "I was worried I'd find an old woman under all that hair, but the summer has been so hot."

"Oh, not at all. With that long, beautiful neck? Uber sexy!" Vicki laughed and then shook her head. "No, wait, that's a rideshare these days, not a compliment. Hmm…I have it…a hottie with the body."

"That's what I said," added Meg. "She's a badass."

Kim laughed again and remembered how she believed her long hair gave her a touch of youth. After years of heavy waist-long braids, she found herself frightened to sit down in the salon chair and let it all go.

But when the hair stylist finished and she looked in the mirror, she couldn't look away. Her neck, which had always been one of her favorite body parts, transformed into a long, graceful pedestal for her head. She stared, not at an old lady in the mirror, but at a powerful woman. A powerful black woman.

"Yes, that's me...sixty-two-year-old badass."

Meg slipped past Kim and headed out the door to her car. Stephanie held open the gate as she returned with two more pizzas and a tall slender gift bag.

"Hey, thanks. I appreciate it. And welcome to town. I hear you just moved from Seaview PD."

"Word travels fast."

"Without a doubt. Here"—Meg held out the arm with the pizzas—"take a piece. I think the top one's pepperoni."

As Meg walked back into the cabin, she heard Sam say, "Oh, really, a little bird talked you into this impromptu party? Hmm..."

Vicki's white skin blushed bright amber as three faces all turned to her. "Can't imagine who that was." Not able to meet Sam's gaze, she kept her head down and filled the wine glasses. Chuckles spread around the room.

Kim said, "There's no denying it, Vicki, you're caught."

"Yup," said Meg, "with that glowing, red face? Your cheeks almost match your hair."

Kim said, in a stage whisper, "If red *was* the color of her real hair."

Vicki pointed at Meg. "Now wait a minute. It was her idea to just show up without warning."

"We couldn't have you bolting on us, could we?"

asked Meg without a bit of remorse.

"I suppose the constant cop cars coming and going from my house was a giveaway that something was up." Samantha laughed and thanked them for the food. As her eyes skimmed the table, her gaze landed on the tall gift bag. "What's this?"

"Open it," said Meg with a grin.

Sam reached in and pulled out a twelve-year-old bottle of Glenlivet. She arched her left eyebrow as she gave Meg a pointed look. "Wine and whiskey? Well, now it *is* a party."

"Meg figured you could use it," said Vicki as she handed around the glasses. "But let's start with the wine."

Then Sam held up the beautiful *Liatris* plant. "And a plant too? Look at those purple spikes. What a great summer bloomer. Thank you. *It's gorgeous!*"

Meg smiled and nodded. "I read your glowing article about them in *The Chronicle*, so how could I not bring you one? If Aunt Dot doesn't let you plant it in the garden, it will be fine in a pot on your sunny back step."

"Kim," Sam asked, "speaking of summer bloomers, how's your summer off going, Professor?"

"I wish it was off," said Kim as she rolled her eyes up to the ceiling.

Sam looked confused, and then her eyes widened. "No!…you didn't…they talked you into teaching the summer session?"

"You got it," said Kim with a long sigh. "Anthro 202. What I was thinking, only the Lord knows. Just one class, but still, what a pain in the ass. Why did I ever let them talk me into coming back?"

When one of the big state colleges partnered with the local community college in Astoria to start a combined satellite campus, Kim got the call from the dean of her old Anthropology department to return to teaching. She, of course, gave them a long list of demands in the hopes they would move on to another professor. But to her profound surprise they said yes to it all. They offered her the best graduate student she could hope for, Lisa Hoptowit, to run the labs and help with coursework, and a flexible part-time schedule with a pay raise.

"Money, my friend," said Meg, "that's why. Miss POC-PhD."

At that Kim laughed. Meg's words didn't offend her. She did refer to herself as a POC-PhD, but she never let that levity be mistaken for a dismissal of her skill and dedication. Back in the eighties when she entered college, a woman of color stood out in a discipline packed with white men. The years of fieldwork and research it took to earn her doctorate came with a level of respect in anthropology circles, she not only expected, but knew she deserved. And over the decades, women of all shades and backgrounds continued to make huge strides in the field in which she liked to think she played a small part.

"A return to retirement is looking pretty good right now, huh?" said Sam with a grin.

"Ugh, don't even talk about it," said Kim, as she rubbed her smooth, shaved neck. "Don't think I haven't been kicking myself. Lecturing? Undergrads? Ridiculous! And students today? What a bunch of little pricks they all are. Rich or poor, black or white, they all think they're so damn special. I've heard every sob story as to why they can't get their work done on time, and in every class there's a sea of bent heads scanning their damn cell phones. Not a one of them understands how fucking lucky they are going to a college like—"

"She's ranting again," said Meg as she moved to the far side of the table.

"And in the end—" Kim ignored Meg and went on. "—most of them will get business degrees, not become anthropologists or archeologists. Is Anthro 202 really going to help these complaining underachievers? In my day—"

"Honey, in our day," said Vicki, "we did what a teacher told us to do for fear of their wrath and our parents when we got home."

"No kidding," said Meg. "In fifth grade I once tried to hit a boy with a rock at recess who was pestering me and my friends, and I was sent—not the boy, mind you—I was sent straight to the principal's office. I spent the rest of the day frickin' petrified of what would happen when I got off the bus and my mom found out."

Laughter erupted around the room.

"You, a boy, and a rock?" asked Kim with a wide grin. "Now that I can see."

As the laughter subsided, Kim went on. "Mmm, I miss retirement. I reveled in it. The time I spent getting my little house just the way I wanted it. The joyful nesting. I'm an idiot."

Everyone agreed, filled their plates, and made their way to the tiny living room. Vicki and Kim sat down on the sofa while Sam rolled her desk chair to the coffee table.

Kim stared over at the dining room table and asked, "Meg, what in the world are you doing?"

Everyone turned to see Meg with one arm out of the sleeve and up inside her Blooms & Blossoms Garden Center T-shirt. "It looks like there's a fight going on under there and you're losing."

"By my watch," said Meg, now with both arms stuck under her shirt, "it's bra-off-thirty." With a final tug, Meg held up her 36B cup for the group to see and with a satisfied smile said, "Whew, there, that's better." She then hung it over one of the table chairs and put her arms back through the sleeves of her shirt.

"Meg!" said Kim, while those who still had their bras on laughed and shook their heads. "Do you have no shame?"

"Nope. And if you were hot flashing with this level of boob sweat, neither would you."

Meg plopped down on the overstuffed recliner that matched the couch. She tucked her stocking feet under Sam's coffee table and reached for a piece of pizza. She wore bright colored socks covered with cartoon shovels, spades, and flowers. Her muddy work boots sat outside on the porch. The nursery owner came straight from the garden center and didn't have time to change out of her uniform top and dirty jeans.

Socks, Sam thought. *Again? Why am I fixated on socks?* She pulled her gaze away from Meg's feet, and as she looked around at these incredible women, tears began to peck at the backs of her eyes.

When she moved here, she told herself to keep her head down and just exist. She never intended to make any real friends. She held everyone at arm's length and tried to survive each day. At first it worked. She moved to town in mid-June. An ideal time to be overlooked and ignored by the locals and tourists. The few hundred people who lived in Cove Beach year-round found themselves far too busy in the summer to care about someone new in their midst. Those who didn't own a shop in town worked in one. The rest moved to the beach to retire. Since she had little in common with those retired, she enjoyed the anonymity.

But by October things changed. On a visit to Crooked House Books, on a stormy day when the wind howled and the rain slung itself sideways, Sam found Vicki all alone in a wing backed chair cozied up to a roaring fire which glowed from inside a big, basalt rock fireplace. The bookstore owner introduced herself to Samantha, waved her into a seat on the well-worn sofa, and asked, "Who's your favorite writer?" Two hours later Sam braced herself against the gale, as she walked back to her cabin with her arms wrapped around a bag of books and an invitation to join the book club.

"So, what the hell is going on?" asked Meg. The words brought Samantha's thoughts back into the room. "Are you up shit creek or what?"

Vicki sputtered and almost spit her wine on Kim, while Kim sat silent for a split second before she cackled with laughter.

"Leave it to you, Meg, to just blurt it out," said Kim as she rolled her eyes up to the ceiling.

"What? Why tiptoe around it? Enough small talk. Somethings up, so let's just get down to it. That cop isn't sitting out there in Sam's driveway because she had nothing better to do on a Friday night."

Meg then picked up another piece of the Mediterranean pizza and took a bite. As everyone began to talk at once, Sam chuckled and put her hand up.

"Stop. Meg's right."

Through a mouth full of sun-dried tomatoes and kalamata olives, Meg said, "Ay oh ay ham." Then to Sam, she added with a nod as she swallowed, "Thank you very much."

Sam grinned and said, "I can't tell you everything, but…"

She then went on to explain what she could about the situation. Colin and Jess asked her not to release any details about the new letters, but if she wanted to tell them about her former identity, that came down to her choice. Sam decided she wouldn't tell anyone her birth name, but she would give these friends the broad strokes of the killings on campus and how they appeared to be starting again. The three women stayed quiet throughout, and when Sam finished, the room remained silent.

Meg cut through the silence first. "Fuck-a-duck! Are you kidding? That's the craziest thing I've ever heard."

"So, all this bitching and moaning about being a professor, the undergrads, summer school I was going on and on about," asked Kim, "you…?"

"Understand completely," said Sam. The tension in her shoulders began to unwind. She found it a relief to finally tell her story to someone other than a cop. "And I know you won't believe this, but I miss it every single day."

"Sam," said Vicki in a soft voice with both concern and confusion on her face, "we had no idea."

"I believe," said Kim with an inquisitive stare at Sam, "that was the point. Correct?"

She nodded her head and felt the tears again as the

sadness returned.

"Yes. I needed to find a place and lie low. I didn't want to leave Oregon, but I knew I couldn't stay in Chinook. Even a move to Portland seemed too close to campus. The press, the reporters, you know. Then the story went national. It was all too much to stay, to…" Sam's words trailed off at this point. Her shoulder sagged at the thought of the old memories. She reached up and wiped the moisture from the corners of her eyes as she cleared her throat.

"And they still can't tell you why you're the one being targeted? Why this lunatic is fucking with you?" asked Meg.

"Nope." Sam thought back to all the theories, the most prominent being her book deal to write a mystery novel. The letters and killing started soon after she signed a contract with Upton Press for a work of fiction. Jessica asked her not to discuss any scenarios outside of the detective team, so Sam kept this to herself.

Meg and Vicki began to talk at once. Sam's eyes darted from each of them as one question after another hurtled toward her. This time Kim put her hand up. "Stop! Sam has told us what she can, and let's leave it at that."

"But," said Meg. Kim gave her a stern look. "No. You're right. Sorry. It's just one hellofa story."

"I'll change the subject. Meg, how is your staffing trouble going?" asked Sam.

"Oh, Jesus, don't get me started." And as Sam hoped, Meg put down her slice of pizza and launched into a tirade about her summer help.

"Lois, you guys know Lois my landscape

designer," Meg said as she waved her arms and pointed at the air above her head to emphasize each of the next five words, "is sixty-seven years old!" Meg flung out both arms and continued before anyone could respond. "And probably doesn't weigh more than 115 pounds dripping wet. And," she went on, more to herself than the women in the room, "I catch her lifting the heaviest bags of soil I sell while my two young backs are nowhere to be seen? Such bullshit! Mark Todd, they are *not*. Another minute of teenage angst and I'm going to pull my frickin' hair out. Those two boys are on borrowed time. And... Oh... Oh...and get this, we had a come to Jesus meeting last week, and I had to slam the Sunset Western Garden Book down on the desk just to get their attention. I tell you, it's like I'm not even there. Like I'm invisib—"

At that moment three loud knocks on the door made them all jump. The laughter stopped, and Meg leapt out of her chair to stand between Sam and the front door.

"It's just the changing of the guards, you guys," said Sam with a chuckle as Vicki and Kim rose from the sofa and began to gather around her. Sam got up and went to the door. "But I appreciate the effort. Come in, Officer Bennett."

The same man from the night before entered the room. Stephanie stayed on the porch. Sam ushered him in and said, "This is Officer Tim, everybody. Be nice to him." She then stepped outside to say good night to Stephanie.

"Just here to take a quick look around," said Tim with a smile as he raised his hands to the group of women to show he came in peace. "No need to stop what you're doing. I'll be in and out in a minute."

Kim pointed straight at Meg, raised her eyebrows, and cocked her head. "Leave it," she said in a low voice.

As the officer disappeared through the kitchen, Meg met Kim's gaze. With a wicked smile and a sly wink, Meg said, "You know me so well." Vicki and Kim rolled their eyes and shook their heads at the garden center owner who stood there braless with a smear of dirt on her cheek.

As Tim returned, he accepted a piece of pizza from Vicki and wished them a good night on his way out the door. Meg turned to the group.

"Please, if you're going to be in and out, make it more than a minute."

the spectrum of autism. He expressed a quality you find in academic geniuses. Somehow people like Paul lacked the ability to read a room or understand the daily social interactions of people. She paused for a moment and tried to remember if Paul held an advanced degree. She never thought to ask.

Marlene's face stayed stern. "He looks like a guy who could get obsessed, you mean?"

Now Sam's smile dropped.

"You think he might have gotten obsessed with me?" She shook her head. "No, no, the police did a detailed background check on him the first time. He had an alibi and"—Sam put up a hand to stop Marlene before she jumped in—"the alibi for the first killings wasn't from his mother. Given what we just heard, he couldn't have been in Chicago in June."

Just like he said in his interview, he did come into her office to say goodbye on her last day at Duniway, but his inability to read social cues left them both in an awkward situation after he made a clumsy attempt to kiss her. She decided the chief didn't need to hear this story.

"What about this mention of theater students? Any of that set off alarms?" asked Marlene.

"Hmm, it feels like something could be there. But once again, am I creating the link?" Sam sighed. "I just don't know."

While they both waited for the next interview to start, Sam said, "Thinking of the theater, can I ask how the meeting with Liz at The Gull went? Or am I not allowed to ask?"

"You can ask. But not much to tell. Her background checks out. She moved to Cove Beach early in the spring and hasn't taken a real day off since the summer season started Memorial Day weekend. Been working on and off with a playwright for the season's production, but nothing seemed unusual."

"Whew, that's good to hear. I don't know what's got me thinking about performances. I guess at the time I must have seen the articles in the student paper Paul talked about."

"Just curious, was there anyone else in the theater back in May when you interviewed—?" Marlene stopped as the large monitor lit up. "Whoops, looks like we are back up and running."

Sam stared at the screen as memories from her PhD days pushed in just like when she saw Paul. But this time her heart didn't soften, nor did she feel pity. As Priscilla Greene sat at the interview table and stared at her through the screen, Sam's jaw clenched and her back straightened.

Paul looked his age, and the five additional years showed on his face. But to see Priscilla left Sam in a complete state of shock. *She hasn't aged a day. How is that possible?*

In a flash, Sam worked through the timeline in her head. *If I had just turned forty when I started at Duniway and met Cilla...everyone called her Cilla back then...don't know why, she never liked being called Cilla...you could tell...then that put her in her late twenties, or maybe thirty?...so, I got my PhD and then taught...a total of...hmm...twelve years?...so, she must be what?...over forty?...forty-two?*

Her blonde, straight hair—in a classic bob cut— looked the same, and her white skin remained flawless. The tailored floral-print dress stopped an inch above her knees and fit her slim body to perfection. She carried a large, bright red designer bag and wore vivid yellow high heels that matched the flowers in the dress.

As a PhD student, Cilla never fit the stereotype for an English Lit academic. *But really, did any of us?* thought Sam. Movies and TV always show men in tweed jackets with leather elbow patches, and women in either frumpy cardigans and thick-rimmed glasses, or flowy skirts and scarves.

Bob lived in khaki pants and wrinkled oxford button-downs with the sleeves rolled up to his elbows. Alicia stuck to the more traditional silk blouse and slacks, while Sam got away with jeans and Birkenstocks. Never once did Priscilla wear anything other than dresses or skirts with designer labels on campus.

Alicia, Bart, and Sam paid for their post-grad studies at Duniway through scholarships, financial aid, and hard work as TAs. But money never seemed to be a problem for Priscilla. The scuttlebutt in the department claimed family money paid her way. She grew up in the wealthy Lake Oswego area of Portland, went to a private high school, and then earned her undergrad degree from an expensive ivy league college. After attending an ivy-league school like that, her PhD application to a small backwater like Duniway didn't make any sense to anyone.

"I'm happy to help," said Priscilla, with a look of concern on her made-up face. Samantha couldn't remember a time when Priscilla didn't have on makeup.

"Whatever I can do to help find who did this to Cornelia. I can't believe it, I really can't. I had just talked to her that morning, before she was…" At this point she broke off and pulled out a tissue from her purse. She then dabbed with care at—Sam suspected—her dry eyes.

"Yes," said Jessica, "tell us about that morning. "You said you were in your office early on Wednesday?"

"Yes, I was going to meet with Cornelia to discuss the Chicago conference and wanted to go over the notes she'd emailed."

"Did she call you or did you call her?"

"Let's see." She paused to think. Her eyes drifted up to the ceiling and then back down to Jessica's face. "I talked to you on Tuesday about how to reach her at the conference and then I called her that night to find out what time her plane was going to land the next day. And then we talked Wednesday morning before her flight."

"And you didn't speak or see her after this point."

"No. She just said she would see me in the office that afternoon. She was going to stop off at her apartment first to unpack."

"And where were you when you spoke to her?"

"If you mean Wednesday morning, then that was about seven and I was already at my desk at Upton."

Priscilla, like Paul, reached for the bottle of water Jacob placed in front of her. She, unlike Paul, opened the bottle and took a drink without bothering to reseal the cap. As she pursed her lips around the bottle, Sam could just make out the fine lines of age creased with her thick makeup. *Ah*, she thought, *that's how it's done. Spackle it on as thick as you can.*

"You live in Chinook, is that right?"

"Yes. Close to downtown, by The Old Grange

Pub."

"I understand you have worked for Ms. Cowan," said Jacob as he pretended to look through his notes, "about, let's see, eight years? Does that sound right?"

Jacob's dark blue eyes looked up from his notepad at Priscilla through long, thick eyelashes. Her attention pivoted to the young officer, and her body shifted. She abandoned the straightforward stance she displayed with Jessica and now became more engaged with Jacob. She leaned in, made eye contact, laughed a little too loudly at his jokes, and played with her hair. Sam shook her head, crossed her arms, and seethed.

Then almost as soon as the anger flashed, so did a happy memory of that same party she and Marlene talked about after Paul's interview. She remembered Priscilla's performance being so like this one. Except the victim of her attention had been Quintin. Cilla attempted to flirt with him most of the night while Quin gave Sam looks of panic and at one point even mouthed "*help me*" when he distracted her with some old first edition on their bookshelf.

A small tear formed in the corner of Sam's eye when she remembered Quin's arms around her waist and his lips on her neck as they slow-danced in the kitchen after everyone left. She'd said to Quin with her head on his broad chest, "Just want you to know, it's not fair. You and Miss-Aren't-I-The-Perfect-PhD-Candidate having sex on top of the coats in the spare room while I was stuck entertaining the guests."

He looked down at her and guffawed. "What! I barely got out of there alive. You were no help at all, leaving me stuck without even a snake bite kit. With those acting skills, she should switch to the Theater department. And that perfume, ugh, what is that? I almost had a sneezing fit." He then swung her out and back into his arms.

Later that night they each whispered in the other's ear, "Thanks for loving me," before they both drifted off to sleep.

As Sam watched Priscilla continue to babble, she tuned out the interview. She let her mind drift to the days in the TAs' office and to what Bob told her at the end of her first day. After Alicia and Priscilla left the small office they shared, he turned his swivel chair around to face her and said, "Just a word of advice. Don't say anything in here you don't want all over campus. One of us"—Bob jabbed his thumb over his shoulder toward an empty desk in the corner—"loves to drag out your entire life story, then tell everyone about it with their own...um...let's say artistic spin."

Office politics always played a huge role in university life. The large state university Sam attended for her master's degree, before her acceptance at Duniway, seemed rampant with it. Priscilla's phoniness came as no surprise. Sam found at least one in every office. But as time went on, Sam came to understand how Priscilla's perpetual lying and gossip could be dangerous. Dangerous because everyone seemed to know and let her get away with it.

Several months later, Sam and Bob discussed it again at length one night over a few beers at a local bar close to campus.

"So," said Sam when they sat down. "Is she the dean's niece or something? Sleeping with the college president? Why does the department chair put up with her?"

"Not sure. It's like she's a rich closet klepto, taking a diamond ring here and a bauble there, and everyone just ignores the behavior. We had an admin like that at the paper."

Sam smiled. Bob had a newspaper story for just about every situation. She found Mike Campbell to be the same way.

"Craziest thing. She wouldn't stop taking the sticky notes and denying it. I don't mean one or two packets...talking two and three cases at a time. Finally had to fire her."

"Do you think the department chair even knows?" Sam asked to move the subject back to Cilla.

"Maybe, maybe not. Either way, she's clearly here to stay, so best we keep our heads down and you go get yourself tenure, and I'll get back to the newsroom, as fast as we can."

And that's what they did. That spring Bob finished his PhD and got hired at *The Northwest News Tribune* as the metro editor. Samantha and Alicia worked for another year to finish their advanced degrees, and Priscilla, to everyone's shock, dropped out after the fall term. Samantha didn't see her again until they nearly knocked heads in the hallway at Upton eight years later. Cilla gushed about seeing Sam again and said something preposterous about the two of them "doing lunch" before she walked away.

Shocked to find she reported to Cornelia as her managing editor, Sam asked CC about Priscilla when they met to discuss her textbook.

"Oh, I know," she said with a wave of her hand. "A conniving, backbiting little bitch."

Sam's eyes narrowed, and her face became red.

"Then why do you keep her at Upton?"

"Relax. Don't get your panties in a bunch." CC smiled and laughed at the look of shock on Sam's face. "Because I *know* she's a conniving, backbiting little bitch. It's when you don't know who you're working with, then there's real trouble. If you got outta this backwater town, you might know a few things about the way the world works, my friend.

"I use her skills—a damn good organizer—to keep me on track. No imagination, of course. Nothing original about her but, meh, that's what my writers are for. But one thing she and I had to have a long chat about were her mistakes."

"You mean she made a lot of them?"

"Hmm, some, not a lot. Everyone makes mistakes, especially when they're new. But no, it was the blaming game I couldn't take. There was always a reason why something didn't get done, and it was never, ever her fault. I won't have that. That sort of horseshit is what puts everyone at each other's throats."

As Sam now sat in the Cove Beach Police Station and watched this woman from her past, more memories bubbled and churned in her mind.

...tragedy...cast of characters...real life—harder than fiction...what's so special about you...conniving...ran away...made the connection...liar...nothing ever her fault...no imagination...nothing original...the theater...socks...was she liked?

Sam's body jolted upright as her phone rang and vibrated in her back jean pocket. "*Jesus!*" she yelled out.

Marlene's head snapped around. "You all right?"

Sam waved the cell phone now in her hand. "Sorry, sorry. Just my phone." The chief gave a sigh of relief, and Sam answered her cell.

"Colin? Hi."

"Hi, do you have a minute to talk about the notes we found in CC's office?"

"Sure, just watching the interviews, but go ahead."

"Oh, yeah, right, the interviews. You know what? Let me scan all of this paperwork and send it to you. Take a look and see if anything jumps out at you."

After printing out the notes Colin sent, Sam made her way through the pared-down rejected submissions going back to 2013. The summary sheets contained CC's short, concise, and straight-to-the-point notes. Those notes, of course, got cleaned up by the office manager before the rejection letters went out to protect the tender egos of the fledgling writers. However, CC's raw notes scribbled all over the margins of the manuscripts didn't hold back.

Things like...*Jesus Christ, have you heard of spellcheck?...really, another legal drama? That might work if you had ever been in a courtroom!...going to add punctuation at some point? ...I'm just going to shoot myself now...give me something new...WTF?...it's all been done before...*

Without any real idea of how to tell who might be a threat, Sam decided to see what jumped out at her as she waded through the pages and people. After about twenty minutes, the list shortened to three possible writers. One in particular received some harsh notes from Cornelia. Devon Dexter.

Sam couldn't explain why she landed on Dexter. Perhaps the Portland address, listed only as a post office box, raised a red flag. She didn't know. But a lot of people used PO boxes. Still no physical address bothered her all the same. She texted the name to Colin as a suggestion, along with the other three.

But then a fourth rejection caught her attention. A writer by the name of Kyle Douglas. She sat there for one brief, stunned moment then grabbed her phone and called Colin back. In a few minutes she explained the email in her in-box and Kyle's connection to Cornelia. Colin assured Sam the Portland PB would question the writer as soon as possible.

Sam hung up and shot a glance at the monitor in time to see Jessica and Jacob finish the interview. As Priscilla got up, her left arm knocked her designer bag onto the floor. Like a choreographed dance, she pressed her knees together and balanced on her high stilettos. She then tucked her skirt hem behind her knees and crouched down to gather up the detritus that tumbled out of the bag.

What a gentleman, thought Samantha as she rolled her eyes when Jacob leapt up to help. *What a good little actress.*

A sudden "Oh!" escaped from Samantha's throat. *This was just like in the bathroom at The Apex*, she thought, *but something doesn't fit. What is it?*

Chapter 20

August 24 – Cove Beach, OR

Now back in her cabin, Sam felt wrung out. The clock read SAT 3:22 PM and the only good night's sleep she could remember happened Thursday after she knocked back a dropper full of CBD oil and two cold tablets. She worried a nap might make sleeping through the night impossible, so she resisted her pillow and decided to walk to the end of the beach path. She promised herself to stop right before it sloped down the dune toward the shoreline and not leave herself exposed on an open public beach.

As Sam stepped out of her cottage, a shiver danced across the bare skin on her arms. She reached back through the door and grabbed her lightweight fleece zip-up off the coat hook. With each step she took down the beach side of the dune, she became more enclosed in mist. As she stopped at the bottom of the path, she could just make out the beach access sign a few yards away.

"Wonderful fog!" she whispered and smiled to herself.

"Portland must have hit a hundred," said a deep voice. Sam jumped at the sound through the fog but then relaxed as a tall figure appeared to her left.

"I'll take it, Ted."

A broad-chested man walked up to her in a navy-blue company sweatshirt with the logo *Ted Rosi Construction* across the front in bright white lettering. He also wore a pair of heavy carpenter shorts, the same mahogany brown as his hair, and a pair of Teva sandals.

Sam first met Ted while he repaired a section of broken fence between her yard and Aunt Dot's. Dorothy's not so subtle attempts at putting them together over cups of tea while he cut and crafted new pickets gave them something to laugh about. But at forty-eight, Ted had been placed by Sam in the he's-too-young-for-you category.

They now bumped into each other around town: the grocery store, Dave's Tavern, and on the beach. Each time they met, she found it harder to look away from those deep, blue eyes. And if that didn't test Sam's resolve to the limits, his olive skin, even more radiant with a summer tan, made him a definite distraction. "He's one good-looking man," Kim liked to remind her whenever they went out for drinks. She pushed down memories of Meg's more salacious comments about when Sam would be seeing him naked and turned her attention back to the conversation.

"Me too. Nothing like a good fog-out. Especially in August. I've had enough of inlanders. Fall can't come soon enough."

"I like this little trick of weather out here. When Portland hits, what? A hundred degrees? All that cool air and moisture gets pulled inland and we fog-out at the beach? Nice little secret nobody tells you about."

"Shh," whispered Ted with his index finger pressed into his upper lip.

Sam laughed. "Don't worry. To watch all the

tourists jump in their cars and hightail it out of town? I'll never tell. Let them drive down the beach and torment some other poor locals."

"No kidding. When I work downtown, all I hear about as they walk by is how the prices are too high, the stores closed too early, the weather's too cold, or bitching there's no place to park. Then go to Seaview, I say, if you want cheap crap and an arcade. I tell you Labor Day can't come too soo—"

All of a sudden, a golden flash appeared out of the fog, and Sam felt two weights shove into her lower belly. She cried out, teetered backward, and windmilled her arms to stop her fall. She stayed on her feet but stumbled into Ted.

"Whoa! I've got you." His arms circled Sam's waist and held her steady. For a moment they both stood still, and as their bodies hovered close, each of them could feel the warmth of the other. The familiar fragrance of Ted's patchouli soap lingered in the air between them. *God, he smells better than I do.*

He then dropped his hands and shouted into the mist as he reached down and made a grasp at a collar.

"*Gordon, off*! Sorry, Sam! Sorry, sorry, sorry."

Sam relaxed and then started to laugh as her heart banged against her chest. *No mad killer on the loose*, she thought with relief.

"Well, hello, Gordon. Are you taking your human out for a walk?" Sam chuckled at the happy face of the big golden retriever whose sandy front feet now pushed on Sam's thighs. His tongue and tail wagged as he hopped up and down with little intermittent barks of joy. The pungent smell of his doggy musk and wet fur rose in waves as he jumped back and forth.

Ted shouted again. The anger in his human's voice brought his four feet down to the ground this time. But not to be deterred, Gordon now proceeded to pick up and drop a wet, sandy ball at Samantha's feet over and over. Gordon lived his life with the assumption that everyone understood the international dog signal for "toss the ball."

Sam laughed, scooped up the soggy ball, and gave it a good throw through the fog and down the beach. Gordon raced to retrieve it. Ted apologized again.

"No problem at all," Sam replied with a giggle as she bent down to brush the sand off her wet jeans and wipe the dog's drool off her hand. "You know I'm secretly in love with Gordon."

As Gordon returned in triumph, Sam leaned down to scratch behind the old golden dog's ears. The dog attempted to nudge the ball back into her hand again and again.

"If he bothers you, just push him away. He's been a pain in the ass like that since he was a pup. Nothing I do stops him."

"Oh, I don't care one bit." Sam crouched down onto one knee. "Do I, Gordon? Nah, there's always time for a good scratch. Someday you and I are going to run off together, aren't we?"

Gordon abandoned the ball and sat down with his eyes closed in ecstasy. He leaned his whole weight into Sam's hand as she scratched his ears and rubbed his head. His tail swung back and forth like a flag snapping in the wind, and his tongue lolled against his cheek.

Ted looked down at Gordon's shameless behavior and laughed. "That's good news. I may run away with you after what happened the other day. He went barreling into some woman on North Beach, and I thought she was going to call the cops."

"No!"

"Yep. I think he thought it was you. It's about the same time in the morning we see you out walking. She really did look like you until we got up close." Ted went on to say that he hated to do it, but he might have to put Gordon on a leash until the season was over.

Whoa, stop the presses! Ted knows what I look like from a distance and what time I walk on the beach? Something about that gave her tingles in places that hadn't tingled in quite a while, except maybe when she heard Colin's British accent on the phone. She blushed bright red and dipped her head down to meet the gaze of the dog at her feet.

"Anyway," Ted said as he reached down and rubbed Gordon's head, "he's just wound up because I put in a few hours' work on a cabin in midtown and this is his first time out of the house since morning."

Sam stopped listening. Her eyes landed on the skin above his left ankle. She never saw Ted work in shorts, so he must have changed out of his work pants before heading to the beach. She could see the elastic imprint on his skin where his crew socks would have slumped down above his work boots. *Socks!*

Sam stood up and shook her head.

"Oh my God," she whispered.

"Sam? Are you okay? What is it? Sam…?"

"Could it be that simple?" Sam whispered again. "We've been—*I've* been looking at this all wrong."

Chapter 21

August 24 - Sunset Highway, OR

The drive started with the sun high in the sky and a warmth on the dashboard. But now only a few miles from Cove Beach, darkness closed in as the shadows lengthened and a mist rose. A chill moved through the car, and long fingers reached out to turn off the air conditioning. In the passenger seat lay an envelope of yellow parchment with a red, wax seal.

The driver's hand moved from the temperature controls to the envelope. As their fingers caressed the seal, their mind went back to how this all started. It began as a hobby—a fantasy—in those first few years. With every injustice and denied admiration for their intelligence, an idea grew from an intangible dream to something alive and vibrant. As the years passed and career success provided the means and opportunity, a plan solidified.

The killing of those three students came off without a single mistake. They placed such trust in someone they never took the time to know. A little charm and a good story made it easy to gain access to the house. The students didn't have a clue when they answered the knock on their door on that third visit. The little spaniel put the cherry on the top. *Nasty, smelly thing,* the driver thought. *It drooled on my leather shoes. Well, I took care of that.*

But the first kill months before the students, the driver could only describe as perfect because that murder no one even suspected as murder. Even now a body lay buried in the ground believed to be the victim of bad luck. No ties to one of those mundane mystery novels, just a beautiful, simple death. No one knew the truth. But it didn't have the intended effect, so other bodies needed to follow, and they needed to get Anna Jean's full attention. The next letter explained it all. The driver hummed along to the classical music that filled the car and thought, *And won't her world come crashing down?*

****

August 24 - Portland, OR

Colin glanced out of the window of the townhouse to see a dry, hot Saturday afternoon. He found Portland's summer heat brutal compared to the cooler coastal weather of Bournemouth. As he strolled through the park to the nearby bar and grill, he looked forward to something he would not have even considered back home, air conditioning. Here everyone seemed to have it, and he could understand why. *One hundred degrees?* he thought. *Bloody hell.*

The neighborhood spot catered not to students, but to the locals, and he liked the idea of a quiet pint in a cool pub with a chance to watch a real football match. American football still eluded him, but a couple of cops at the station told him there wouldn't be any televised games until fall. This gave him hope the bartender might be agreeable to finding a Premier League game on one of the sport's channels. Just as the bar came into view, his cell phone vibrated in his lapel pocket. He looked down at the caller ID and smiled.

"Oh, hello, Samantha. So, have you solved the case yet?" He chuckled to himself.

"Yes, but no way in the world to prove it."

"What!" Then he relaxed and said, "You're winding me up."

"No, there really is no other explanation for the lie and the socks," she said, as if it made complete sense.

"Lie? Socks? I have no bloody idea what you are talking about!" He wondered if long exposure to this woman would drive him bonkers in the end.

As he pivoted and made his way back down the sidewalk to his apartment, Sam's tumble of words spilled into his ear. She explained what she'd seen and why she believed one little lie solved it all. When she finished, Colin stood on his doorstep astounded.

"So, if you are still at the office and can get them back to the station, then—" said Sam in a rush.

"Office? No, none of us are at the office today."

"What do you mean?"

"Those interviews were done yesterday."

Colin could hear Samantha's fast-paced breathing over the phone.

"Samantha, are you oka—?"

"Yesterday? That means no one is...you aren't...?"

"I thought Chief Porter told you. Because of the tech troubles, we taped them but didn't stream to you until today. Those interviews finished about one yesterday, and then we all went home."

Colin pressed the phone to his ear as Sam said in a low whisper, "When you said no sitting in on the interviews until Saturday, you didn't mean the interviews were postponed until Saturday. You meant *I* wouldn't see them until Saturday. Oh no!"

As if she had taken a punch in the gut, Sam gasped. "I made a big mistake."

"No, sorry, I didn't mean to confuse you. Are you—"

"Colin, listen to me. I know who the killer is and who the next victim will be, but there's no way you or Jess can get out here in time to stop it."

"Stop what? Samantha, you aren't making sense."

"D! Can't believe I didn't see it before. I've got to go."

"D? What are you talking about?"

"I don't have time to explain. Just write down all the victims' names in order of their deaths. You'll get it."

"Sam?" Colin looked down at his cell phone. "Samantha!" His screen read, Call Ended.

Before he could call Samantha back, his phone rang. "Yes, Detective. Glad you called. I just got off this rum call from—"

"Save it!" said Jess as she cut him off. "I'm on my way to your apartment. We may have caught a break." Then Jessica hung up too.

Chapter 22

August 24 - Portland, OR

Jessica's tires squealed to a stop in front of Colin's townhouse about ten minutes after their call. With no time to spare, she stayed double parked in the middle of the street and texted from her car. Colin jumped in, and Jess pressed her foot to the floor. Colin slammed the passenger door shut as the car lunged forward. As the police car raced down SW Park, Jess filled him in.

"Okay, so get this," said Jess, "Neilson's alibi for Alvarez's murder. Remember he said he was on vacation over those dates in June? So, guess what? He was in Cove Beach."

"Cove Beach? Now that's a turn up."

"Isn't it? And you won't believe—or maybe you will, who knows, you see a lot—his hobby is acting. He's been in college productions and even does a little playwriting on the side. So, that's where we are headed, Neilson's place. Calhoun should already be there with a uniformed team."

"Playwright? Why does that sound familiar?" Colin's brow came together, and he tapped his fingers on his thigh. "But that doesn't put him anywhere near Chicago."

"True, but I still think that was a hired job. Too clean."

"To what end? Why would a killer, who by all accounts is enjoying killing, hire out one of the murders? Sorry, Jessica, that just doesn't fit the profile."

"It could if we dropped this idea of the mystery murderer theory and look at Alvarez as a murder unto itself."

"You think Sam is wrong about the killer using her old lecture topics?"

"Hmm, not wrong, but overreaching with Alvarez. She's trying to make a theory fit the facts."

"Right, let's go down that line. What about Paul for the other murders?"

"Pretty much like everyone else. How do you prove someone wasn't home alone or driving to work?"

"And now Kyle Douglas and Devon Dexter are thrown into the mix. Rather unlikely coincidence— Douglas and Cowan attending the Chicago conference. Where are we with him?"

"Calhoun is on it but couldn't track Douglas down today. It's the weekend. It's harder. He left messages from the information the writer gave to Sam in that email. The guy lives in Chicago but with family ties in Portland. So, yes, a red flag goes up."

"And Dexter?"

"Nothing on him at all but an old blog where he talks about the book he was working on years ago." Jess turned toward Colin and cocked her head. "The one Cowan ripped to shreds by the way."

"How can we take anything we know about them as true? Everything we have so far is online with emails and then just cell numbers. Do we even know if Dexter is a man or a woman? Or who Douglas is for that matter."

With a snort, Jess looked back at Colin and rolled her eyes. "Devon? Kyle? Kind of a giveaway, don't you think?" She paused for a minute with a frown as she slowed the car down to stop at a red light. "I guess Devon could go either way, man or woman, but Kyle—"

"Not if they're pen names."

"*Holy shit!*"

"Quite! So, now you really need to hear about my call with Samantha."

As Colin finished, Jessica asked, "Has she lost her f-ing mind?"

"Completely lost the plot, without a doubt, but that's what she said."

Just then Jessica's phone rang. She jabbed at her cell phone as she pulled away from the intersection.

"Detective Noguchi? Neilson's not home, and he's not picking up his cell. I made a call to campus security to check his office, and they confirmed he's not at work. Said the whole building was empty being a Saturday in August."

Jess hung up with Jacob and stayed quiet for a few minutes. With a slight nod of her head, she reached out and tapped a button on her navigation screen. The light on the top of the cop car flashed, and the siren blared as she rerouted the car.

Colin braced himself against the seat as the patrol car made a wide swing around the next corner. "So, where are we going?"

"Cove Beach." Jess didn't take her eyes off the road. She didn't want to miss the Hwy 26 exit. "If Sam *is* right, she may be dead by the time we get there, and the killer long gone. Colin, please get Chief Porter on the phone for me."

But when Jess looked over, she could see Colin's eyes fixed on a scrap of paper in his lap.

"Colin? Did you hear me? Please give Porter a call?"

He didn't look up as he jotted down the victim's names in order of their murders, as Sam said he should. Now, as he looked down at the list, his whole body went still.

"Bugger me! She's right." His head swung toward Jessica. "D! And you're also right. We aren't going to make it in time."

****

August 24 - Cove Beach, OR

Samantha left Ted and Gordon on the beach and bolted up the dune path to her cabin. She could hear Ted's voice, but she didn't stop to explain. As she reached the top of the trail, her phone rang. Before she could answer it, she barreled straight into two tourists headed down to the beach.

"Oh! I'm so sorry. Are you okay?" She waited only a moment for the bewildered couple to nod and then sped across the top of the dune.

"Mike, sorry, can't talk right now."

"Kid, wait! I've got something for you about the Alvarez murder."

Sam slowed but didn't stop. "That's great, but I really—"

"No! You are going to want to hear this. My contact just told me there were hairs found in the woman's hand, they think from the killer."

Mike went on to tell her more, and when he

finished, Sam said, "That really is great, but I know who did it, and there's no time." Then she said with a sob, "And…Mike, thanks for everything."

The line went dead. Mike tried to call her right back, but the call went straight to voicemail. His next call went straight to the Cove Beach Police Department.

****

Sirens blared and horns blasted as two police vehicles and a fire truck whizzed by Meg at Blooms & Blossoms. She turned off the valve to the water hose and watched as the whole cadre headed out of town up to the highway. Through the windows she recognized Chief Porter in the lead with Tim Bennett in the car right behind her.

"It's a big one." Meg rolled her eyes and shook her head.

"Yeah, I just heard about it on the scanner as I drove in," said Mark Todd's mom, Donna, as she walked up to the sea of deep purple salvias laid out in tidy rows by Meg's feet.

"Hey!" Meg put the hose down and wrapped her tanned muscular arms around the small wisp of a woman. "What are you doing downtown on a Saturday afternoon with all these knuckleheaded tourists, you crazy woman?"

"Just finished the lunch rush at The Windswept and thought I would treat myself to something pretty on the way home."

Just then a third police car zoomed by the two women. Officer Dean sat behind the wheel. She had the sirens turned up full in an attempt to move the slow-moving traffic out of her way.

"Yikes!" said Meg. "This can't be good."

"No, not good. The report said big crash on 101, multiple cars, the whole deal. Happened at the bend just before the second exit. All officers called to the scene with volunteer first responders and the fire trucks from Seaview. Traffic's blocked all the northbound lanes into town. You can still drive south from Astoria and Portland but at a crawl."

Meg heard a slight quiver in Donna's voice. "Oh shit! Sorry, Donna." Meg's brain just registered the passenger in Stephanie's patrol car—Mark.

Donna put a hand on Meg's forearm. "Don't worry. It's what he loves and all he's ever wanted to do. And I trust Marlene to take good care of him."

Meg could hear the pride in her voice but also a hint of fear for her only child. "She damn well better! Mark's one of the few kids giving me hope that the whole world isn't going to hell on horseback with this next generation of slackers, whiners, and internet nitwits."

Meg stuck her thumbs over her shoulder. "Look at those two boy wonders over there."

Donna looked behind Meg to see one teenage boy with his phone in one hand and a hose in the other pointed at a row of pink Japanese anemones. Water overflowed the side of the pot. The other boy sat on an overturned bucket.

"Do they not realize that I can see their lazy asses from here?" Meg sighed. "Or do they just not care? I'll never know. You tell that kid of yours he has a job, anytime he wants to come back to work for me."

Donna picked out a salvia from the row closest to her feet, and they both walked together to the register. After Meg boxed up the perennial and left the warm greenhouse, Donna turned to make her way back through the vine covered, wrought iron arbor to Sitka Street. She dipped her head to duck under the brilliant, red trumpet vine flowers that dangled down in full bloom.

"Wait. Don't go out the front. It'll take you days to get to your car with all those mouth-breathers on the sidewalk. Here." Meg pointed to a path alongside the nursery's storage shed. "Sneak out the back way."

After Donna left, Meg turned to confront the two boys. But before she took the first step, she stopped and pulled out her cell phone. The time read 3:45.

No! she thought, *Oh fuck!* She jabbed at the phone as she darted back inside the greenhouse. "Come on, come on," she muttered underneath her breath as she waved her arms to get Lois' attention and listened to the phone ring.

"Shit! Voicemail." Meg then dialed a different number as Lois walked up to her with a puzzled look on her face.

"Kim! Thank God! Are you home? We have trouble."

"What's up?"

"It's Samantha. There are no cops in town, and it's almost the top of the hour."

"What are you babbling about?"

"Remember what Sam told us the other night? An officer would be checking on her every hour. There's a big crash on 101, and I've just seen every police car and officer, including the chief, leave town."

"Damn!"

"Exactly, can you get to her house right now? She's not answering her phone."

Meg's eyes fixed on Lois as the older woman held out her hand and mouthed the word, "Go!" Meg placed the store keys into her palm and gave Lois a grateful smile.

Meg then said to Kim, "I'm right behind you."

****

Sam ended the call with Colin just as she reached the top of the dune. She paused to catch her breath and whispered, "Well, now what am I going to do?"

The voice in her head answered. *You have to catch a killer before they kill again. And you need to move. There isn't much time. She'll be home any minute. Get next door. NOW!*

Sam dashed down her path and ran to the big house. Once on Dorothy's deck, she cupped her hand against the glass and peered through the sliding glass door. She hunted through the gaps in the vertical blinds for Dorothy's figure inside the house. She knew the historical society didn't stay open past three on Saturdays, and Sam's clock read a quarter to four.

Sam pounded on the door and cried out, "Aunt Dot! Aunt Dot!"

Sam ran farther down the deck toward the small pool to look into Dot's kitchen window. The sweat gathered beneath her collar and under her bra even though a cool breeze began to blow onshore. Up on top of the dune the fog thinned, and the sun strained through the mist chased by a dark cloud.

"Doesn't look like anyone's home," said a familiar voice. A voice she heard just this morning. From around the far side of Dorothy Dixon's house came the one person she knew it would be, Devon Dexter dressed in a black hoodie and running pants. "Pity, this bullet isn't really for you."

Chapter 23

August 24 - Dorothy Dixon's Garden - Cove Beach, OR

If no other event this week made Sam feel like a character in her own mystery novel, this moment did. *I'm dialoguing with a fucking killer*, she thought. *This would be hilarious if I wasn't so goddamn scared.* She remembered writing a scene like this for her own doomed novel. *If I ever do write another mystery, I'll remember to write in more fear and nausea, and less bravado. I'm fucking terrified.*

"Guess we'll just have to wait until she gets home. But you being here must mean you figured it out? Good for you. Curious, what gave me away, AJ?" the calm and collected voice asked as an arm leveled a gun chest high at Sam. "Oops, sorry, what gave me away...*Samantha*?"

The satisfaction in the voice oozed out like an oil spill on the surface of the sea. The lack of regret or remorse in the words smothered the small triumph Sam took in being right about the killer and the last victim. At this distance, Sam could see the gun and the killer's steady hand. The hand didn't tremble.

While Sam moved fast to put the small pool between her and the killer before the gun appeared, she now understood a moment too late that this trapped her at the far corner of Dot's yard. Only a rickety picket fence and the cliff face of the dune stood behind her. She could jump the short fence in one quick motion, but she didn't see how she could slide down the dune before the gun went off. As her eyes darted toward the house, the killer moved off the deck and onto the lawn. This move blocked her access to the beach trail.

Sam's eyes fixed on the gun, and they refused to look away. The wind picked up, and Sam heard a rustling and faint popping sound off to her left. The dark-blue sheets on Aunt Dot's clothesline snapped in the wind.

A part of Sam wanted to laugh out loud at such a common, everyday thing, but she knew if she opened her mouth, she would sob. Just that morning, Sam took an overflowing basket out of Dot's arms and asked her, "Do you think it's a good idea for you to be carrying a heavy load of laundry outside and reaching up to hang them on a clothesline when you have a perfectly good dryer in the house?"

The older woman laughed and said with a shrug, "Darling, when you've always done something, well, you just keep on doing it."

"AJ, hello," said a voice sticky with sarcasm as they waved their arm in the air. "Killer with a gun here. What gave me away?"

"Your sock line, Priscilla." Sam made the statement and stopped.

Her mind then began to churn up a thousand ideas at once. No clarity. No single thought...*shit!...isn't extreme stress supposed to give you pinpoint focus?...something like that, right? ...shit!...shit! ...shit!...another as seen on TV myth ...complete bullshit!*

"My what? What are you talking about?"

"The morning of CC's death. You said you had gotten the call and came directly from the office." Sam parceled each word to draw the story out as long as she could.

With a shake of her head, the slender, blonde woman lowered the gun a few inches and began to wave it around as she talked. "So? What did that have to do with my socks!"

"Not your socks, your sock *line.*"

"That's absurd. You're just making this up to buy time."

You have no idea, thought Sam, but she went on. "If you'd been at your office all morning and only left to go to the crime scene, then why were you in gym clothes, probably like the ones you're wearing now, before you showed up in your dress and high heels?"

Priscilla took a quick look down at her black joggers and then back up at Sam. Her eyes narrowed. "What do you mean in my gym clothes? What makes you think I went to the gym that morning, and why would it matter?"

"I have no idea if you went to the gym or ran five miles through downtown Chinook. Just in all the years I've known you, I can't remember you in pants and tennis shoes. Except one time I came back to the office late at night to see you headed to the campus gym dressed in workout gear. Your sock line told me that you lied about where you were, and that was the lead I followed. You're the killer of all these people."

As the last word left her lips, Samantha felt a sickness rise in her stomach and pain grip her heart. *All these people*, she thought. *Dead.*

Priscilla's face darkened before she bellowed, "What are you talking about? What does all this have to do with a line in my socks?"

"No, not a line in your socks, you weren't wearing socks at the time."

Sam sounded exasperated. Her old professor's voice began to creep out. *This isn't a fucking teaching moment!* she told herself with a shake of her head. *Just stay alive!* The fear now caused Sam's hands to shake, and an intense urge to pee her pants pulled at her groin.

"The line your socks made on your skin, the indent. When I dropped my backpack in the bathroom in the lobby of CC's building on Thursday, I didn't know it was you in the stall next to me. But as I bent down to pick up my stuff, I was eye-level with your ankle and those four-inch-tall stilettos you were wearing. It meant nothing at the time. My mind just registered shoes and socks. But today as I watched your interview, I saw the heels you were wearing when you dropped your own bag. I didn't make the connection right away, but then about a half an hour ago on the beach I had it. You had to have had anklets on sometime before you arrived at CC's apartment, or else the skin around your ankles would have been smooth. So, you were lying, and there had to be a reason why."

Priscilla tossed her head back and shrieked, "You got all that from a wrinkle in my skin? Nonsense! I'm not buying it. There had to be something else."

"Nope, that was the start, and then it all just sort of fell into place from there. Your next big mistake was giving the police CC's rejection file. Why didn't you take yours out? Why would you take a risk like that?"

"How could there be any clues in that file?" Priscilla asked as Sam watched in disgust at the smugness on the woman's face. "Those were know-nothing writers who wouldn't have the balls to cross the street on a yellow, let alone plan the perfect murders."

Priscilla seemed to forget she held a gun in her hand. She waved it around while she jabbed and pointed at the air as she talked like she didn't realize what the damn thing could do. Sam's whole body flinched every time the gun swung in her direction.

"And that is where the arrogance took over." Sam took a risk with this confrontation but hammered on. "You thought you were so protected you put your own name on the list assuming no one would piece it all together."

Priscilla raised her head and the gun.

"I never submitted anything to Cornelia," Priscilla said in a voice filled with confidence. "You're completely delusional."

"Not in your own name." Sam inched her way toward the clothesline. "But under your pen name, when you first began at Upton years ago, you did. You submitted three manuscripts. The last rejection letter came from CC herself, one week after you started as an assistant editor. You thought you were too clever by half. Not every editor keeps a rejection file, but CC did. Yours were there. The copy of the rejection, addressed to Devon Dexter. D!"

Priscilla lowered the gun a few inches and then whispered to herself. "I was so careful."

Sam could see the confidence on her face fade. She pressed her advantage. "Having all the Dexter mail delivered to you at a post office box told me I was right."

"Why?" Priscilla now screamed with a sudden rage.

This fury took Sam by surprise. It caused her to wince and take a step back. That motion roused Priscilla, and her eyes fixed on Sam like a raptor as it stalked its prey.

Sam now stood with her back to the sheets. She glanced down to notice a large, flat-head garden shovel and pair of long-handled tree pruners propped against the fence. *How would those two things help?* Her mind went blank, then with still no clear idea, she thought, *But they're better than nothing.*

"Why?" Priscilla spat out the word for a second time. "Lots of people have PO boxes. Why would that matter?" She raised the gun again, but this time her hand shook. This provided Sam with no level of confidence. One nervous twitch might cause it to go off.

"Yes, they do," Sam said, "I do in Cove Beach because we have no delivery in town. All mail has to be picked up at the post office. But that isn't the case for most people. Most people use home addresses, and that got me thinking about why this person decided to not have mail delivered to their physical address…you, sending me letters here to a PO box…seeing Devon Dexter had a PO box…no explaining it really…with that and the socks, it just made sense."

Priscilla then pulled herself up upright and straightened the sleeves of her jacket with slow deliberation. The movement made Samantha more frightened than she'd been in her entire life. A calmness came over Priscilla's features, and a smile filled her face. Sam could see a decision had been made.

"You really are one of the stupidest women I have ever met. I knew it the minute you walked into the Lit department. Standing there in your ridiculous Birkenstocks and dumb look on your face. No one else saw it, but I did. And all those idiot undergrads just eating up your lectures about a bunch of commonplace mystery writers. What a bunch of bullshit, while I was doing serious research on the classics."

Sam never once heard Priscilla swear or behave any way other than as a cutesy little fashion doll. As she stared at this woman in front of her, it started to make sense. She could see how this person, whom the world believed had it all, committed these murders. The precision of the plan and the execution left Sam speechless for a moment. For all she hated about Priscilla, she stood before a brilliant mind. Her high level of control almost pulled it off—five years ago— and over the past few months.

"And Cornelia? She was the worst, falling all over herself to publish your prosaic textbook. A bigger fool than you. Working for her was a joke."

Priscilla's thoughts went back to Cornelia, the crème de la crème of them all. Planned down to the last detail. She remembered the time and research it took to find the perfect drug derived from a plant. Strychnine and belladonna which both came originally from plants were easier to obtain than one would think. The former would get the job done, but only the latter would get the attention.

A smile played on her face as she recalled setting the stage in CC's Apex apartment. Once again, the cops wouldn't see the artistry of the cards on the table, the way her arms and hands seized at just the right angle. The frozen look on her face, with the added macabre element of the laugh track on the editor's own laptop. It could only be described as flawless. She'd staged the Holmes' story to perfection.

No one else knew CC had taken the earlier flight back from Chicago. This left plenty of time to talk CC through the final minutes of her life. She had been incredulous, snide even. Of course, CC would never have believed anyone could get the drop on a seasoned New Yorker like her.

"You've got to be fucking kidding me!" Cornelia bellowed as she sat and listened at gunpoint. "You? You're the one? Unbelievable! What did I ever do to you?"

And then Cornelia heard it all. The years of rejection letters. The years of struggle without recognition. The years of watching mediocre writers rise to fame with their formulaic, cookie cutter plots. The years of writing only to hear the most infuriating critiques. And the one that triggered it all from some crappy little university press—*It's all been done before. Give me something original.*

Priscilla's face now filled with joy when she thought about the last words Cornelia heard before the muscles in her body seized. *Originality? Does that really matter when you realize you're about to die?*

"You know, CC was wrong about you, Priscilla," Sam said in a reckless attempt to delay her inevitable death.

Priscilla roused herself from her happy memories and said, "Yes, she was in many, many ways, but you tell me why you think so."

"Remember when I ran into you in the hallway at Upton about…what?…seven years ago? How surprised we were to see each other?"

Priscilla hesitated for a moment. "Yes, that was the first meeting for your shitty little textbook."

"Right," Sam agreed. She decided the last thing she wanted to do was argue literary content with a crazy person.

"So, when I got to CC's office right after we met, I asked her about you being on staff. While she told me you were a great organizer, she also said you had no imagination. Nothing original about you, CC said. But I have to disagree.

"You planned some incredible murders. The way you staged each scene to see if I would catch on to the stories. Nothing but imagination. Three murders, four stories. Impressive. And you hit all the biggies: Ellery Queen, P.D. James, Sherlock Holmes, Agatha Christie…you recreated them all."

"Don't forget the Ratcliffe Highway Murders," Priscilla said with a broad smile on her face.

"Oh, right, the true-crime mystery."

The Highway Murders. As Sam remembered those poor students—drugged then killed with such violence along with the little dog—the grief overwhelmed her. She could feel herself on the verge of tears.

"Yes. I'm surprised you figured them out with your unremarkable intelligence. Teaching The Art of Detection. Please, what a disgrace for our English department." Priscilla snorted. "I spent my whole career working to get to the top, wanting a full professorship, research grants, to get published, and you come in and take it all. Oh, I told them too, those idiots in charge, but they wouldn't listen…everyone just loved you. *You!* A short, fat, moronic little bitch. No dedication, no discipline, no real intelligence, no—"

"Well, the stupid, little bitch figured you out, didn't she?" said a quiet, clear voice from behind Samantha. The two women facing each other both jumped at the sound. Sam wrenched her head over her shoulder to see the outline of a person behind the sheets on the line. The fog and mist disappeared in the last few minutes, and the summer sun now dropped behind the clothesline. She couldn't make out the person's face through the dark cloth, but Sam knew the voice. Her mind worked to decide if what she knew would be a good thing or a bad thing. But she did feel a tingle of hope and then trepidation.

Priscilla swung the gun off to Sam's right and pointed it toward the sound.

"Who the hell is that? Get out here right now!"

"I think not," said a voice by the far side of the house, while at the same time a pair of arms reached from behind the sheet and pulled Samantha out of sight.

In that same moment, Priscilla swung the gun behind her. She searched for the location of the new voice. Her eyes scanned the deck and yard. It appeared empty.

"Don't say a word," a voice whispered into Sam's ear. She stopped, stock-still.

Priscilla's voice became light. She chuckled. "Oh, so you've made friends, have you, Anna Jean? Isn't that adorable, but they are just as stupid as you are because I can see two of you behind the sheet." Then came a harsh laugh. "Your shadows, brainiacs."

"But maybe they aren't the only ones, dickhead,"

said a voice from Dorothy's deck, clear and loud. This time, without hesitation, Priscilla fired straight at the sliding glass doors. The sound of the gun and shattered glass filled Sam's ears.

She now understood who had come to her rescue. She reached out to pull back the sheet. She couldn't let anyone else get hurt. As she lunged forward, two arms came down around her.

"Don't move."

A dark cloud blocked out the sun.

"Oh, Kim, what have you and M—?" came Sam's whispered sob as a cool, dry hand wrapped over her mouth. Sam reached behind to steady herself against the fence and felt two handles. *Which one is going to help us*, she thought, *shovel or pruners? Which one can save both our lives? Clearly, I'm losing my fucking mind if I think either one of them will stop a bullet! Shit, this is really it!*

Sam's eyes fixed on Priscilla's outline. She couldn't see every detail through the dark sheet, but Sam could at least keep her body between Priscilla's and Kim's.

Then Sam saw what she had dreaded from the moment Priscilla had pulled the weapon from her purse. The outline of Priscilla's right arm began to rise as the rain began to fall. Sam reached out and grasped the space behind her. Then her eyes caught movement behind Priscilla. Sam could see more people inside the big house. At that distance, she couldn't make them out, but with the glass broken and the sun gone, the windows no longer reflected the light.

Don't get distracted! Stay focused on the woman with THE GUN!

Priscilla's fingers then reached into her jacket pocket and drew out a yellow envelope with a red wax seal. "Before you and your friends die here today, you should know there's one murder you didn't figure out." She waved the letter back and forth. "Do you want to know how your precious Quin died? It's all in here."

Sam froze. Kim's arms tightened around her as Sam's chest spasmed with pain and a sob jumped out of her mouth. *No, not Quin. Not my Quin.*

"No, you know what? I don't think I am going to tell you." Then Priscilla tucked the letter back in her pocket. "I'll let your next of kin read about it instead."

Samantha's face flushed hot, and her mind now burned with a fury she'd never imagined possible. As she fought to get free from Kim's strong, solid grip, Priscilla brought the gun up to shoulder level. She braced it with both hands, outstretched her arms and pulled the trigger.

"*The shovel!*" screamed a voice. Sam's body reacted. She ducked down and grabbed the handle while at the same time she swung the head of the shovel around to cover her face and chest while her body blocked Kimberly. She didn't know if the words she heard were real or only in her head, but if they were real, then the whole neighborhood heard her scream.

The sound of the shot echoed around the garden, while at the same time the yard became filled with voices and more gunfire. For Sam, everything moved in slow motion. She felt a powerful force drive her back into the fence. The shovel flew up and over her head and tumbled down the cliffside and out of reach. Her head spun, and her ears rang with a barrage of bangs. As her ribs slammed against the picket boards, she gasped for air. She opened her mouth, but no air would move in or out of her lungs.

What's happening? she thought, as her body rebounded off the fence, jerked sideways, and knocked her off-balance. Now tangled in the sheets, Sam grabbed and pulled at the fabric to stop herself from falling. Her head pounded, and her lungs burned. The clothesline held for only a moment and then gave way. From her own momentum she stumbled forward, and out of the corner of her right eye she saw a flash of Kim's arms as they reached out to her.

She heard a dull splash and then felt a rush of cold water enclose her body. The water streamed down her nose and filled her throat. Her vision filled with little sparks of light as she gasped again for air, and then— nothing.

Chapter 24

August 24 - Seaview Memorial Hospital - Seaview, OR

"You're kidding me! A graceless belly flop?" Sam laughed, as she sat up a little taller in the uncomfortable hospital bed. Her whole body ached. She shook her head and said under her breath, "I thought I was dead."

In the past hour, Sam's friends had filled her in on what happened after her tumble into the pool.

"So did we," said Marlene, with a big grin. "You weren't breathing, so technically you were…well…for a moment anyway…"

"And no wonder. You sucked up half the pool," said Meg. "Ha! Took all of us to get you hauled outta there. I wanted to borrow a sub-pump from Ted Rosi to clear your lungs, but first responders wouldn't let me."

Laughter then filled the packed room. Vicki and Kim stood on one side of the bed, Marlene and Stephanie on the other by the door, while Meg hovered at the foot. Aunt Dot sat at the head of the bed with her hand held tight to Sam's. A lump formed in Sam's throat as she gazed at the fearless women who saved, not only her life, but Dorothy's.

"And, Professor, what made you think a shovel was going to protect you from a bullet?" Kim asked as she swung her head back and forth. That brought more laughter.

"No idea." Sam shrugged her shoulders and raised both hands, palms up. "I was just lucky to be thinking at all at that moment. It was all there was, so I used it."

"That was why you went into the pool," said Marlene. She then pointed across the bed. "Kim reached out to stop you as you fell forward. Luckily, it was enough of a grab to slow you down. You could have missed the water entirely, gone all the way over the side, and cracked your head wide open on the metal filter."

"But the bullet hit the shovel, right?" Sam asked. When the room went silent, she looked over, first at Kim and Vicki and then Meg. Both just shook their heads and grinned. Aunt Dot patted Sam's hand. Then the room filled with giggles and snickers.

"What? What is it?"

Marlene said, as she tried to hide a smile, "No, Greene's bullet went wide. Dean had already fired her weapon." The chief paused for a moment, as chortles and chuckles filled the room. "Um, so…ah…what happened with the shovel was—"

"You swung the damn thing up so hard toward your face, you knocked yourself out," Meg cut in with a hoot of laughter. At that point no one could keep a straight face. Everyone in the room gave way to fits of laughter.

"Stop it!" cried Sam as she held on to her rib cage and coughed. "Don't!"

It took a minute before she could speak again. "So, I just imagined a heroine's ending, did I? No going out in a blaze of glory?"

Sam gave them all a pained smile as she rubbed the

warm lump in her hairline. She then gave up and put the back of her hand to her forehead and said, *"Oh, the final humiliation."*

After the room had become calm, Sam picked out her next words with care and asked, "And, Priscilla? Is she…?"

"No, not dead." Marlene's smile disappeared, and her face became stoic. "She'll live to stand trial." Her face then softened back into a small smile, and her voice held a note of pride as she pointed to Stephanie. "Our crack shot over here was able to take her down without doing too much damage."

Stephanie blushed and said as she looked around the room, "I just didn't want to hit any of you. So, I went for her thigh, and she dropped pretty quick." She patted her own right leg. "A shattered thigh bone is beyond painful, that much I know."

Sam opened her mouth to ask the million questions in her head, but before she could speak, the doctor came in and cleared the room. Aunt Dot stayed seated and kept a tight hold on Sam's hand.

With a warm smile, Dr. Suzanne Olney looked up from her tablet and took two long strides to stand beside the bed. Even though she didn't look old enough to legally drink, Sam put her in her late thirties with straight, black hair held at the base of her neck with a colorful hand-beaded clasp.

"Good evening, Samantha. My plan was to keep you overnight, but by the looks of it there are plenty of people to watch out for you. And the celebrity of the hour probably wants to sleep in her own bed, I'm guessing, eh?"

She didn't pause for an answer but went on,

"Everything looks good, and we've had enough of you all shouting the place down. Hospitals aren't for having fun. Haven't you heard? There are sick people here. So, out you go!"

Over the next few minutes, the doctor went over the things Sam needed to know about her injured ribs, her lungs, and the knock to her head. "You have antibiotics for the fluid now clearing in your lungs. The ribs? Luckily, they're just bruised. No internal damage. But you'll just have to tough it out—I'm afraid—through the healing process. Sorry. I've given you a low-dose pain prescription to take the edge off. With ribs some pain is good, keeps you from overdoing it. I don't see signs of concussion, but no computer screens, devices, or epic novel reading for this week just to be safe. Nap, rest, and let all these troublemakers wait on you."

"Praise the Lord and pass this woman her purse!" Meg said with a big grin from the doorway. "You're sprung!"

With instructions to return to the emergency room if she spiked a sudden fever, had trouble breathing, headaches, or vomiting, Sam sat down in the wheelchair and headed for the door. It looked like a parade as she rolled down the hall with two police escorts while three women laughed and chatted along behind.

Chapter 25

August 25 – Samantha's House, Cove Beach, OR

Colin, with a large bundle of flowers in hand, gave a light tap on the weatherworn front door. As he waited on the tiny porch, he looked out at Sam's small garden. The leaves on the plants looked polished and new after last night's heavy rainfall. A moment later an older woman with kind green eyes opened the door and said, "Yes, dear?"

Before he could answer, the older woman said, in a low, quiet voice, "Oh, now look at those lovely flowers. Come in, come in." She stood back and let Colin into the little living room. Dorothy whispered introductions and then said to Colin with a smile, "Please keep your voice down, dear. Samantha is napping."

"Oh, sorry. Not to disturb. If you could just give her these flowers and let her know I stopped by."

"Nonsense," said Dot. "You're one of those from Portland, aren't you? Dear, you didn't just stop by. You made a real effort. Just have a seat, and I'll put the kettle on." At that, Aunt Dot turned and disappeared into the next room.

As he sat down on the sofa, Colin heard voices in the kitchen. He'd hoped he hadn't awakened Samantha. He'd asked Jess to drop him off in town before she headed back to the Cove Beach station this morning. He found a florist stand inside the little market, and then he walked the three blocks to Sam's house.

Jessica and Marlene needed to meet before interviewing each of the women involved in yesterday's confrontation. Since Colin's time as a consultant ended in a few weeks, he left the strategy meeting to the two detectives.

After the shooting, Priscilla had been flown to the state's medical school and largest hospital in Portland. Now out of surgery, she would recover with armed guards placed in her room and on the ward.

Colin heard the tinkle of china and looked up to see Dorothy with her hands gripped around a tea tray chock-a-block with cups, saucers, a teapot, and a plate of biscuits. Colin jumped to his feet and reached for the tray.

"Colin? Hi. Could you please grab the tray?" asked Samantha from her bedroom.

"He's already got it, Sam, dear. I'm fine." Aunt Dot beamed at Colin. "Good, British manners. See, I told you," the older woman called over her shoulder. "American boys just don't have the upbringing the good English ones do."

"Too right!" he said with a wide grin.

As he put the tray down on the coffee table, his eyes landed on a white ceramic pitcher covered in blue polka dots half filled with water. Dorothy took the flowers from his hands, sat down across from the younger man, and began to arrange them into the makeshift vase.

As she made deft work of the arrangement, Dot asked, "Where are you from, dear?"

"I teach in Bournemouth."

"Oh, lovely area Bournemouth, and the town of Poole which is where university is, correct?"

"Yes, right in one."

She smiled at the finished arrangement and then picked up the teapot.

"Where are your people from?" She held a cup and saucer. "Milk and sugar?"

"Aunt Dot, stop giving the poor guy the third degree. Sheez-us!" Sam said from the far side of the kitchen where she tried to fix her hair in the mirror without being seen. To stay out of sight of the living room presented a challenge in the 550 square foot cottage. "I'll be right out."

Colin laughed. "Hello, Samantha. It's fine." He then turned and gave Dorothy a wide smile. "Yes, please, milk and sugar. I was raised in Shropshire, on the family farm."

While Sam continued to fuss over her hair and wrinkled sweatshirt, Dot continued to find out all she could about Colin Davies. After a few more attempts, Sam thought, *Oh, to hell with it.* After a night of sleeping in fits and starts, she didn't see the point. Her ribs screamed at her as she took slow, deliberate steps over to the kitchen sink. She poured a glass of water and downed one of the small, pink pain pills.

"Ah, now that's a proper cuppa, Mrs. Dixon. Cheers. I've been served some dodging ones since arriving in the States." Colin grinned and took another sip of the hot tea.

"Yes, a certain American tea company has a lot to answer for, if you ask me, dear."

"Hi," said Sam as she came around the corner to meet up with her two guests. "Sorry to look like something the cat dragged in, but if you hadn't heard, yesterday was a bit of a challenge."

"Really? No, no one told me a thing." Colin stood as Sam came into the room.

The smile dropped from his face when he saw her hunched over with one arm around her ribs and the other one against the wall for support. He put down his teacup and reached out to take her free hand. After he helped her hobble to the couch, he and Aunt Dot fussed until Sam lay propped up with pillows and her rib cage supported against the armrest.

"And," said Colin as he turned to Aunt Dot, "I hear you are one lucky lady to have missed all the excitement yesterday."

"Yes." Dorothy chuckled and flushed just a little. "All thanks to Beverly Cole. She cornered me as I locked up the historical society to talk about the garden club's fall harvest festival. Good Lord, that woman can go on and on. I may have to be a bit more charitable with her in future."

Aunt Dot then made mention of the beautiful flowers from Colin as she moved toward the door. She chattered about Ted on his way to see to her sliding glass window and all the things "needing doing" at home. With a final wave, she disappeared. Sam called out, "Thank you," as the door shut behind her.

She turned back to Colin and snorted. "She's nothing if not subtle. Please, sit." Colin then sat down in the seat Dot just vacated. "And thank you. The flowers really are beautiful."

Dorothy had arranged the flowers so that the pale lavender bow fell over the lip of the pitcher just below the greenery. The colorful summer blooms brought a cheerfulness to the room.

The next half an hour or so, they each filled the other in on key pieces of the story. Sam had no idea what he and Jess had uncovered in Portland, and he'd only gotten snippets here and there about what had happened next door the day before.

"When I figured out what you were trying to tell me and realized just how far away we were, I was terrified you were already dead."

"So was I. I heard the sirens but had no idea about the big accident. Meg figured out my police protection was gone and called Kim. Those two are the real heroes of the day."

When Colin looked confused, Sam explained how Kim had gotten to Dorothy's first just as Priscilla arrived. "When she heard voices, she went around the backside of the house and worked her way along the fence to hide behind the bed sheets on the clothesline. Then Meg arrived a few minutes later. She was smart enough to stand in the shadow of the awning alongside the sliding glass doors on Aunt Dot's deck, out of Priscilla's line of sight. Kim and Meg both called the station on their way to find me, but they assumed the police wouldn't make it in time."

"I was completely gobsmacked when I did what you asked and wrote out the list of victims in order. *The A.B.C. Murders*, by Agatha Christie? Well done, you! But I thought the D you meant was Dexter."

"So, that's what gave me the final piece. If Dexter, Priscilla Greene, was the one behind all of this, then she wouldn't be the victim but the killer."

"But how did you know Greene and Dexter were one and the same?"

"Ah, well, CC gave me the final clue on that. I remembered something she had said about Priscilla." Sam chuckled at the memory. "I was even crazy enough to tell Priscilla about it while I was stalling for time—"

Colin cut in. "Bloody clever that was, keeping her talking. Don't know if I would have had the nerve. She was expelled from the graduate program, by the way."

He went on when he saw the surprise on the former professor's face. "Caught lying to her PhD advisor, about you apparently, and they dropped her. When we finally found Paul, he was the one who told us about Greene's poor performance at Duniway. And she had routed Cornelia's phone through the office. That's why no one could reach her in Chicago. All your calls and messages—and Jessica's—were going directly to Greene's cell. She was controlling them all. We aren't sure, but we think she was the one who put your friend on the earlier flight too. No idea what Greene told her, but something got her on the earlier plane. We do know it wasn't Cornelia who changed the flight, but someone in the Upton office."

"Wow!" said Sam, more than a little satisfied to hear someone had finally caught Priscilla out after years of lying.

"But, sorry…go on. What was it Cornelia said to give you the idea for all of this?"

"So, when I told CC about my experiences with Priscilla in the Lit department, she called her a conniving, backbiting little bitch. Shocked, I asked her why she would keep a person like that at Upton. CC had laughed and told me it was because she *knew* she's a conniving, backbiting little bitch."

Sam chuckled again. "Better the devil you know, I

guess. But here's the part of the conversation that really made me think. CC said she kept Priscilla for her ability to organize, to keep her on track. She admitted Cilla had no imagination. 'Nothing original about her,' CC said."

"Give me something original." Colin parceled out each of the four words. "The note we saw in the rejection file."

"Yes, and then she said the next thing that brought it all together. Which I *did not* tell Priscilla, by the way, as she was standing there aiming a gun at my head. I may be crazy, but not *that* crazy.

"Anyway, CC told me she expected her to implode in the next few years. 'Her kind always does,' she said. 'Can't hold it together forever, buttoned up too tight.' Said she knew it in the interview and that a phony's mask will always crack at some point. CC figured she could get a few good years of work out of her and then poof, self-destruction.

"CC was so self-assured." Sam shook her head and yawned.

"She even talked about whether or not there would be a big, dramatic scene at the end. You know, 'and the Oscar goes to' sort of thing? CC even said she hoped she would be there to see it."

At these last words, both Sam and Colin sat in silence for a few moments and thought about how CC *had* been there for the dramatic scene. At least one of them. Sam would never forget the last one.

"I was surprised Priscilla had a gun, though," Sam said.

"Why?"

"Because the final murder in Christie's *The A.B.C.*

Murders is done with a knife. Priscilla was so specific about each killing, I thought she'd have stayed true to the story. But she was losing it, so maybe that's why."

"Oh, she was surely losing it." Then Colin paused and gave Sam a quizzical look. "Not sure if I'm supposed to tell you this, but she had a knife in her purse."

"What? No!"

"Yeah, a long boning knife. Nasty looking thing. Jessica's hoping that once forensics gets ahold of it, there'll be some additional evidence."

"Then, what was the gun for? Was she going to use it to get Dorothy to cooperate, do you think?"

"Probably. We believe that's what she did to get Brignone in the chest."

Sam sat there stunned and thought about all the different ways things could have gone wrong. She'd be in the morgue right now if not for the help of good friends.

"So, this theater angle you were twigging about from the letters?"

"Mmm… What? Oh, that. Must have just been my overactive imagination."

She could feel contentment move around her body. Her ribs still throbbed, but she didn't care. Through the brain fog she thought, *Those little pink pills must be kicking in.*

"We did find a bit of a connection with Paul." Colin then went on to explain the missed information about the student murders and Paul's hobby as an amateur actor and playwright.

"Huh? Well, that's all news to me. Maybe I did read something back then about the students." She put her hand up to her mouth and said through another yawn, "Who knows."

"This may be the completely wrong time to show you this," said Colin as he pulled a folded piece of paper from his lapel pocket, "but I have a copy of the last letter."

Sam eyes caught sight of the paper and stared fixed for a few seconds. Then she shook her head. "I already know what's in it. Priscilla couldn't resist telling me about it before she tried to shoot me."

Colin pulled his gaze away from Samantha's sad eyes and trembling lips to look at the letter in his hand.

"It's about Quin, isn't it?" she asked before Colin could speak.

"Yes. And Cornelia."

Sam wiped a tear from her cheek and then winced as she sat up straighter on the couch. "Tell you what. Just leave it, and I'll work up the nerve to read it later. On my own."

Colin nodded and tucked the paper under the tea tray. His thoughts went to the words he'd read in that letter late last night when he and Jessica went through Priscilla's clothes and purse. While it reiterated many of the things printed in the past letters, it also gave new insight into the killings.

It explained how she'd gained access to Quintin's art restoration lab and soaked his cotton swabs in the extract of the deadly plant, oleander. All restoration projects, as Priscilla learned, start with the restorer repeatedly wetting a cotton swab in their mouth to clean a small test spot on the piece. With the poison in place, she just needed to wait for Quintin to begin his next project and then watch him die. She did make a feeble apology in the letter about the unexpected consequences of him going into a coma instead of a more immediate death.

She believed his death would remove Samantha from Duniway and Priscilla's life for good. But only six months after her husband's death, there AJ sat in Cornelia's office with a book contract for a mystery series. That, coupled with CC's rejection of Priscilla's literary manuscript, lit the match and sparked the inspiration for what she called "the production."

Priscilla went on to explain how the killing of Alicia and Bart served only to set the stage for Cornelia's murder and to destroy Samantha. "Bit players" is how she described them. Once CC died, then the only thing left was to bring Samantha to the edge of the cliff and push her off. Priscilla believed killing Dorothy and revealing the details of Quintin's murder would unhinge her.

As Colin stared down at the tea tray, he could understand why Samantha didn't want to read the letter. Knowledge wouldn't bring her friends back. Knowledge wouldn't bring her husband back.

Colin lifted his eyes and gazed at this brilliant woman reclined on the sofa in front of him. In the past week, Colin found this former professor to be quite adept at deciphering the little, insignificant details to suss out killers, and to have rather good reflexes when it came to dodging bullets.

"Now, what's all this bloody nonsense about socks?" Colin asked with a chuckle as he poured himself another cup of tea. When Sam didn't respond, he glanced up to see her eyes fixed on the flowers in the vase.

She stared at the mixture of zinnias, her favorite annual, and, "Oh!" she gasped. In front of her stood three luminous purple gladiolas with white throats and golden stamens. She couldn't believe she'd forgotten.

"Samantha? Are you all right?" He shifted to the edge of his chair and reached out to take her hand. "Are you feeling ill?"

Sam pulled her eyes away from the gladiolas as she felt his warm hand on hers and smelled the scent of his aftershave mingle with the fresh flowers on the table. Into her mind drifted, *Mmm, cedar and bergamot.*

She gave Colin a small, sleepy smile. "Today's my birthday."

Epilogue

December 15 - Wilsonville, OR

A trim, blonde woman hobbled with some effort down a long corridor, flanked on both sides by two female correctional officers. A long chain snaked from around her ankles up to her cuffed wrists, and a tall brace on her right leg started at her groin and ended with a large boot on her foot. When all three reached the far end, the two officers herded the woman through a series of barred doors that opened and closed with loud sirens and bangs that echoed through the hall.

As they led her into a small room with two chairs placed across the table from one another, she looked up to see a young man in an expensive suit with a tight grip on a leather briefcase. He sat on the side of the table opposite the door. He cleared his throat, and then with a slight quiver in his voice he asked the officers to remove the cuffs and to leave him alone with his client.

"I don't know who sent you," Priscilla Greene said as she shifted in her seat, placed her hands in her lap, and eyed the young man with amusement. *Surely, this kid was in the wrong place talking to the wrong inmate,* she thought. "But I didn't call a lawyer. My overpriced, ivy-league attorney did a fine job of getting me life in prison with not a chance in hell of parole, so I think the job here is done."

"Oh, no, I'm not a defense attorney," the young man said in a stronger voice as he shook his head and stared at her with wide eyes. "No, no. I'm with Decker & Spence."

Silence.

The man went on when Priscilla didn't respond. "The publishing house? Out of New York?"

"I know D&S." Her eyes narrowed as she looked across the table with confusion and suspicion.

"I'm here to discuss a contract." He smiled and pushed a stack of papers across the table.

"Contract?" she blurted out. "I think it goes without saying, I no longer work in the publishing industry. You know that small incident of poisoning my boss, a top editor, along with killing a few other well-deserving members of the public?" Priscilla finished with a snort.

However, she did pick up the papers in front of her and read the first few lines. Decker & Spence carried a roster of best-selling authors from all over the world. A crease began to form between her eyebrows as she continued to scan down the page. The words swam in front of her.

...exclusive contract ...reserving the right ...potential three-book deal ... option to renew...

Her head snapped up to see an eager smile on the lawyer's face.

His head bobbed up and down. "Yes, yes, we would like to buy the rights to your autobiography with first right of refusal for your previous submission of fiction to Upton Press. Now, I understand you don't currently have an agent, so if you would like the time for your own lawyer to go over the contracts, that's—"

Priscilla's ears began to ring, and his words became muddled with the buzz that filled the room. *Can this be happening?* she thought, *I don't believe it.*

As she flipped through the papers to the last few pages, she read the dollar amounts offered for her to write her life story and the advance for the work of literature she submitted years ago to Cornelia, if accepted. She then stopped and looked up at who she now realized must be a novice in the industry.

"Sorry to be the bearer of bad news," Priscilla said, "but it seems you haven't heard about a little group of statutes called the Son of Sam laws. A person convicted of a crime can't make a profit from their crime or crimes. The royalties from my autobiography would go to the families of the victims, not me. I won't agree to that." She leaned back in her chair with her arms folded across her chest. "They aren't getting a penny for my story."

The young executive smiled and said, "Oh, we know, but Archer/Dalton Publishing recently took a case to the U.S. Supreme Court on this very issue and won arguing first amendment rights. We feel confident that if this were to go to court, the precedent would stand and be worth the legal fees for what we anticipate in book sales."

Priscilla remained silent, so the man went on. "In the meantime, there's an editor at D&S reading your original literary submission and would like to work with you to publish. Since that work has no ties to your crimes, you are free to make royalties—no advance, you understand—but royalties once the book is making money."

With slow deliberation a smile moved across her

face, and she regained that lethal composure that terrified Samantha by the pool a few months before. Priscilla Greene stared up at the young executive, with a happiness that lingered around her lips and asked, "Do you have a pen?"

A word about the author...

"What in the world are you waiting for?" said the voice in Cyndi Stuart's head as she woke up on her fiftieth birthday. "That mystery novel isn't going to write itself! And YOU, sweetpea, are NOT getting any younger."

So, after years spent as a naturalist and garden speaker, Cyndi dusted off her old Comm degree, left technical writing behind and got to work on short stories, flash fiction, and personal essays. But in secret she tapped away on her first mystery/thriller. Yes, you guessed it, Deadly Yours. The book you just read. The challenge of creating stories from her own imagination, current events, history, and things she might have overheard at the local coffee shop is what makes her happy and where her passion for writing began.

She lives in the Pacific Northwest where she and her husband, a potter and artist, run an artisan business. When not reading, writing, weeding, or pruning, Cyndi can be found hiking, biking, or swimming in the local lakes, streams, and even Puget Sound (in a wetsuit).

https://www.goodreads.com/author/show/1477210 5.Cyndi_L_Stuart

Thank you for purchasing
this publication of The Wild Rose Press, Inc.

For questions or more information
contact us at
info@thewildrosepress.com.

The Wild Rose Press, Inc.
www.thewildrosepress.com